From the Files of

Madison Finn

Read all the books about Madison Finn!

Coming Soon!

From the Files of

Madison Finn

Sink or Swim

By Laura Dower

HYPERION
New York

For Myles, of course

Special thanks to Louise
for making life that much easier

If you purchased this book without a cover, you should be aware that this book is stolen property. It was reported as "unsold and destroyed" to the publisher, and neither the author nor the publisher has received any payment for this "stripped" book.

Text copyright © 2003 by Laura Dower

Volo® is a registered trademark of Disney Enterprises, Inc.
From the Files of Madison Finn and the Volo colophon are trademarks of Disney Enterprises, Inc.

All rights reserved. No part of this book may be reproduced or transmitted in any form or by any means, electronic or mechanical, including photo-copying, recording, or by any information storage and retrieval system, without written permission from the publisher. For information address Volo Books, 114 Fifth Avenue, New York, New York 10011-5690.

Printed in the United States of America

First Edition
3 5 7 9 10 8 6 4 2

The main body of text of this book is set in 13-point Frutiger Roman.

ISBN 0-7868-1735-6

Visit www.madisonfinn.com

Chapter 1

"I just love that tank top," Madison told her friend Fiona Waters as she passed Fiona the tube of sunblock. "Where did you get it? You look so good in purple."

"Fiona looks good in *everything*!" Aimee Gillespie said.

Fiona giggled. "Well, I feel like a fried egg," she said, rubbing on some lotion. "My mom got the top for me at a bargain sale. Can you believe it? Usually I hate everything she picks out for me."

The three friends stretched out on a trio of beat-up green chaise lounges in Aimee's backyard. Madison and her friends had spent the last few mornings doing year-end testing at the school and had spent those same afternoons sunbathing at

Aimee's. Today was the last day of tests, however, so summer vacation was *really* beginning.

"Pahhhh, pahhhh, pahhhh, ROOOOOOOWF!"

On the grass at their feet, Madison's pug, Phin, and Aimee's basset hound, Blossom, panted in an effort to keep cool in the hot sun. It was only June, and already the thermostat was hovering in the high eighties.

"Global warming freaks me out," Aimee commented, squeezing some lemon juice onto the top of her hair. "It's not supposed to be this warm, is it?"

Madison tugged on her T-shirt and pulled up the straps on her bathing suit top. "My mom is doing a documentary on the melting South Pole ice cap," she said, squinting. "She has all these books about it in the house. It's depressing to think that part of our planet is melting."

"What happens to all the penguins if the glaciers melt?" Fiona asked.

"The glaciers can't all melt," Aimee said abruptly. "Can they?"

The three girls sat in thoughtful silence for a moment. Then Fiona leaped up from her chaise lounge and clapped.

"Okay! We can't talk about this anymore. It's too depressing. It's summer!" Fiona squealed. "We're supposed to be talking about other stuff and goofing off and getting tans and . . ."

The two dogs jumped up with her and howled,

chasing their tails around and around in circles.

"Swimming!" Fiona said, grinning. "Let's go swimming."

"It's after three," Aimee said with a groan. "My mom wants me to help her with something at four."

"Yeah," Madison said. "My dad is coming to pick me up soon."

Fiona looked disappointed.

"We can turn on the sprinklers," Aimee suggested. "Blossom loves running through the spray. And we're half wearing bathing suits."

Madison smiled. Phin liked sprinklers, too. He liked to roll around on the wet grass to cool off his belly and back.

Aimee yelled for her brother Dean to help turn on the backyard sprinklers. They grabbed a stack of towels from the Gillespies' basement laundry room and prepared to cool off.

At first the spray felt like hard little pellets, but gradually the three friends got used to the water and pranced across the lawn, cooling off happily with the two dogs.

"This is just like how we did it when we were little," Madison cried, dashing through the sprinkler and sliding on the grass. She landed with a thump and burst into laughter. Her faded jean shorts were completely drenched.

"I can't wait until soccer camp starts," Fiona said, sliding across the lawn in the opposite direction. She wrung the wet out of the bottom of her purple tank top before running through the spray again.

"I can't wait for ballet camp, either," Aimee said, diving into the spray with a carefully choreographed leap. She let the water soak her from head to toe for a moment. Then Madison leaned over and held her hand over the sprinkler, redirecting the water spray straight at Fiona.

"Quit that! HEY!" Fiona yelled. She stepped onto the grass hard and splashed mud and water back at Madison.

"Hey, yourself," Madison said, laughing. By now the three friends were soaked.

Aimee twirled around and screamed to Dean, "Turn off the water!"

The trio ran back over to the chaise lounges and stretched out in the sun to dry.

"Have you decided yet what you're doing for the rest of the summer, Maddie?" Fiona asked. "Last Friday you said you might go to computer camp, but then yesterday you said you were just hanging out."

Madison shrugged. "Yeah, I guess."

"Huh? Guess what?" Aimee asked. "Which is it?"

"I don't know," Madison said.

"Why don't you come to dance camp with me?" Aimee asked. "Or work in my dad's store with me?" Before heading to camp, Aimee was working part-time in her dad's cyber café, part bookshop and part Internet café, in downtown Far Hills.

4

"Get real," Madison said. "I can't dance to save my life. And your dad doesn't need any more help. You have four brothers."

"You'd better decide on something to do before the summer's over," Fiona said. "You'll die of boredom doing nothing."

"Mom's away on a business trip for a week and a half. I'll figure it out before she gets back," Madison said. "I won't die of boredom in nine days, will I?"

While Madison's mom traveled to Australia to meet with some hotshots at Budge Films, Madison was spending the early part of the summer at her dad's downtown apartment. It was fun to stay there. She missed a lot of things about her room in the Blueberry Street house, but Dad's house was special, too. He'd made sure of that. That week Dad even let Madison redecorate her small room with cool patterned sheets and curtains ordered from the latest Boop-Dee-Doop online catalog.

"Maddie, I have an idea. Why don't you enter the library's book-a-thon with me?" Fiona suggested. She was determined to read more books than any other junior high school student—or anyone—in Far Hills that summer. Already Fiona was halfway through reading the fourth Harry Potter book for the fourth time.

Madison shrugged, uninterested. "I'm a slow reader," she said.

Fiona rolled her eyes. "Well," she said, reapplying some sunblock. "It was just an idea."

"Egg, Drew, and Hart all got picked to be junior lifeguards at the pool. They posted the list yesterday," Aimee said. "Now, *that's* a cool way to spend the summer. Hanging out at the pool center, sunbathing by Lake Dora . . ."

"I know," Fiona said, blushing proudly. "Egg e-mailed me as soon as he found out."

"Of course he did!" Aimee said, teasing her friend. She poked Fiona until they were up and running around the puddles by the sprinkler again, careful not to slide on the slippery grass.

Madison felt like rolling *her* eyes. Aimee was so lucky. She always had a million things to do in summer, winter, and all the days in between. Fiona was even luckier. Not only did she have the book-a-thon and then soccer camp to keep her busy this summer, she had a guy, too—even if it was only their friend Walter "Egg" Diaz.

"Want a drink?" Aimee asked. She hurried inside to grab a few cans of soda. Madison and Fiona played catch with the two dogs.

"You'll think of something to do," Fiona said reassuringly.

"Thanks, Fiona," Madison muttered, tossing a stick at Phin.

"Well, you always have us," Fiona said, smiling. "There's always a silver lining—best friends are forever."

"You sound like my gramma Helen," Madison said, smiling back at Fiona.

"Hey, Maddie!" Aimee yelled from the door of the Gillespie house. "Your dad just pulled up outside!"

Fiona threw her arms into the air. "What? You have to go *now*? So soon?" She leaned over and gave Madison a damp squeeze.

"E me later, okay?" Aimee said, rushing over to give Madison a good-bye hug, too.

"Are you guys definitely going to Lake Dora tomorrow?" Madison asked.

"Definitely!" Aimee said.

"Egg said he'll be at the pool center all afternoon," Fiona said. "They have classes there in the morning."

Madison and Aimee shot Fiona a look. They both burst into laughter.

"What's so funny?" Fiona said, spacing out a little bit. "I just said—"

"You know Egg's entire schedule?" Aimee said.

Madison started to hum the wedding march. "Dum-dum-dee-dum . . ."

Fiona blushed a deep pink. "Is that bad?" she said, acting self-conscious. "I mean, I like him. . . . You guys already know that. . . ."

Madison threw her arm around Fiona. "Oh, Fiona," she said. "We're just kidding. Right, Aim?"

"Right." Aimee nodded. "Gee, I wonder if Ben Buckley will be at the pool, too."

"Ben Buckley?" Madison raised her eyebrows. "What made you think of him?"

"I don't know—um—um . . ." Aimee stammered. Now it was her turn to blush. "What was I talking about?"

"Are you in like with Ben or what?" Madison said. "I can't believe it."

"I am NOT in like with Ben," Aimee said. "I was just . . ."

"Ha-ha-HA!" Fiona gave Madison a high five. "So I'm not the only one with a terminal crush?"

"Okay, I admit it. I like him a teeny bit," Aimee said. "But neither of you can tell a soul. I would be so embarrassed if anyone knew. . . ."

"Who are we going to tell?" Fiona said. "Ivy?"

"Ooooh! Don't even say her name!" Aimee wailed.

Madison chuckled. Ivy Daly, also known as Poison Ivy, was their main enemy in school—and out.

"Yo, Maddie!" Dean yelled out from the house. "Your dad is still waiting outside. Hustle it up!"

Madison gasped. "I've got to go!"

Fiona and Aimee helped Madison pick up her stuff off the lawn chairs and shove it into her orange bag. And although she didn't want to leave, the departure was perfect timing. This way Madison could cut out before either friend had a chance to tease Madison about boys *she* liked. Madison currently had a secret crush on another classmate, Hart Jones, but neither BFF knew about it. Only two people knew. One was Madison's online keypal Bigwheels, who lived thousands of miles away. The other was her pug, Phinnie. And dogs don't blab secrets.

Madison snatched her bag and flip-flops and dashed over to the side gate of Aimee's house. It led directly to the driveway where Dad's car was parked. Phin scampered along behind her.

"Later!" Madison called to her friends, waving. They waved back. Blossom let out a little howl.

Dad sat inside the air-conditioned car, listening to classical music. Madison felt like she'd entered a concert hall as soon as she piled into the front seat. The AC gave her chills up and down her spine.

"Sorry to keep you waiting," Madison said, breathless. She pushed the front seat forward so Phin could hop into the back.

"Aw, are you still wet?" Dad groaned, grabbing a blanket from the backseat. "Here, sit on this." He kissed Madison on her forehead and put the car into gear. Phin settled down behind her. He loved the cool air.

"How was your afternoon?" Dad asked.

"Good. The same," Madison said, her teeth chattering a little. "We sat in the sun. Talked. You know. Just like we did yesterday."

"Uh-huh," Dad said, nodding. "Any new ideas about what you want to do for the rest of the summer now that school testing is over?"

Madison gazed out of the car window and sighed. *What to do?* First her friends pestered her and now Dad wanted to know, too?

"I was thinking of joining the circus, Dad," Madison said.

Dad made a droll face. "Very funny," he said. "I'm laughing, *inside*. I just want you to keep yourself active. Is there a sport you can participate in? Some girl group?"

Madison leaned back into the seat and let him fire away with the questions. She had no answers—yet.

They drove on toward his apartment, where he'd prepared a spaghetti dinner for the two of them. Dad loved to cook, which made staying at his place all the better. He served the pasta with sauce onto plates, and the two of them sat down in front of the television. That was another bonus about being at Dad's. Here Madison could watch TV and eat at the same time.

After dinner Dad disappeared into his study while Madison disappeared into her room to go online and check her e-mail. She hooked up her orange laptop so she had immediate access to all the same files and mailbox functions she normally had at home with Mom.

FROM	SUBJECT
✉ Boop-Dee-Doop	Your Order Has Shipped
✉ Bigwheels	Whassup??
✉ TheEggMan	THE POOL

The first e-mail was a surprise. The sheets and curtains she'd ordered for Dad's place were being shipped out via Priority Mail. She could redecorate over the weekend—something to do!

The second e-mail was from Bigwheels.

From: Bigwheels
To: MadFinn
Subject: Whassup??
Date: Tues 17 June 4:16 PM

:-V Is testing over yet? Ours is!! I am SO glad. We leave for horse camp soon. My mom is driving me to this mountain cabin with other kids and we all ride horses all day long. It's supposed to be good for us. Mom always says that about everything. U should be here 2 since u like animals sooo much. We could horseback ride together. Have u ever been on a horse? Well, write back soon and tell me what ur doing for summer. I know it was between hanging at the lake and getting a "real" job. I bet I know what you'll pick—ha ha.

Yours till the Popsicle sticks,

Bigwheels, aka Vicki

p.s. My cat Sparkles says hello.
Well, actually she says meow. LOL.

Madison clicked SAVE. Then she opened the e-mail from Egg.

From: TheEggMan
To: MadFinn, BalletGrl, Wetwinz,
Wetwins, W_Wonka7, Sk8ingboy,
Dantheman
Subject: THE POOL
Date: Tues 17 June 5:01 PM

just saw the wether chanel & it is
like 50% chance of rain that is so
totally BAD. Ok. everyone who was
coming 2 meet me & Drew & Hart @
the pool—if it rains we should now
meet l8r @ the cafe instead. Ok?
Call me if u can't meet at 2. we
have swim lessons in the morning
rain or shine.

Bye, Egg

Madison clicked DELETE. Rain? What was he talking about? It wasn't even cloudy.

After logging off the computer, Madison checked the clock. Mom would be making her nightly long-distance phone call to Madison—and she'd know all the right things to say at a moment like this. Madison got ready for bed and waited patiently for the telephone to ring.

Dad handed her the receiver. "Guess who?" he said, winking.

Outside the bedroom window, a yellow moon hung in the sky over Far Hills. When Madison heard Mom say, "I miss you, honey bear!" into the receiver, everything seemed all right with the world—even just for a split second.

It didn't matter that Madison hadn't yet decided on her summer plans. Something would come along soon—wouldn't it?

Chapter 2

Phin's wiggling woke Madison up from a deep summer sleep. For some reason, whenever they slept over at Dad's, Phin couldn't be awake in the room unless Madison was awake, too. So he parked himself on top of her head and started to wiggle.

Madison opened her eyes and pushed him off. The air conditioner in her room hummed louder than loud, but Madison just lay in bed. Her talk with Mom the night before had been a disappointment—cut short when Mom's film crew interrupted. Thus Madison had gotten no advice on summer plans. She hadn't even gotten a good-bye "hug by phone."

"Maddie!"

Dad marched into her room and opened the shades.

"Goodness! This place is a sty, Maddie!" Dad said.

He was right. Madison was living half out of her suitcase and duffel bag and half out of the permanent closet. She had books she hoped to read piled high in one corner and a mess of CDs piled near a small boom box.

Phin bounded off the bed when he heard Dad's voice. Madison snuggled deeper under the covers.

"Mmmmm . . . go away, Dad," she mumbled. "I'm asleep."

"Ha-ha. Nice try," Dad said. He stood at the foot of the bed, arms crossed. "Your friend Fiona called. Since it's raining, everyone's meeting over at the cyber café. Do you need a ride, or can you walk?"

"It's raining?"

Madison looked out the window. Egg's prediction had come true. The Weather Channel was right. Big, fat raindrops plinked against the glass. There would be no pool today.

"I'll walk to the café," Madison said, knowing it would frizz her hair. But she liked that. Most people hated what humidity did to hair. Not Madison. She liked the additional volume a few degrees—and a little moisture—could add to her hair.

Madison crawled out of bed and stumbled into the kitchen, where she poured herself a bowl of Toasty-Os with dried cranberries instead of plain old raisins. Dad usually had extraordinary kitchen ingredients. Dad's girlfriend, Stephanie, was seated at the kitchen counter, sipping coffee and eating his homemade almond biscotti. She had stopped off at Dad's after an early-morning doctor's appointment.

"Maddie!" Stephanie said when Madison walked into the room. "How are you?"

Madison made a face and leaned over to scratch Phin's back. She still had trouble getting used to the idea that Dad's girlfriend appeared unannounced in the apartment. It had only been a little over a year since the big D, divorce. Did Stephanie always have to drop by?

"I'm okay. Tired. Good morning, Steph," Madison said aloud in a monotone.

"So what's your big plan for the summer?" Stephanie asked, chomping on her biscotti.

What's your plan for the summer? That question *again*? Madison groaned and chewed extra loudly on her cereal.

"We don't have a plan yet for the summer, Steph," Dad said, walking into the kitchen at that exact moment. "But we're finding one this week."

"I could find a plan today if you would both just quit pestering me!" Madison said, her voice sounding an awful lot like Oscar the Grouch. She dumped her breakfast bowl into the sink and scrambled out of the kitchen to pick out clothes. If everyone was meeting at the café, Madison would be seeing Hart

16

and the other boys. She needed an outfit that would say "cute friend with possibilities" loud and clear.

Madison rushed back into the bedroom and threw open the closet.

Moments later, after flinging T-shirts and shorts far and wide, Madison realized that Stephanie was standing in the doorway. Madison knew what Stephanie was doing. Whenever Mom traveled on business, Stephanie liked to act all buddy-buddy. Like she was some kind of robo-Mom replacement Madison never, *ever* requested.

But as annoying as Stephanie could be, Madison had to admit that Stephanie did give great advice—especially about fashion. And she always acted super-nice. And she always took Madison's side. . . .

"That shirt looks very cute," Stephanie commented when Madison pulled on a little baby tee with a camouflage print. "And I'd wear your hair up, since it's raining."

"You think so?" Madison said. She turned around to Stephanie and sighed. "Hey, I'm sorry for being such a—"

"Don't even think about it. I'm not a morning person, either," Stephanie said with a wink. She and her coffee cup disappeared back into the apartment.

Madison decided to go with Stephanie's choice and wear the army shirt with a pair of dark denim shorts she'd purchased at a thrift shop. She laced her high-top sneakers and combed her hair into pigtails.

"Hey, Maddie," Dad said. "Come into the living room for a second. I want to show you something online."

Dad had powered up his high-tech laptop so he could show Madison a Flash Plug-in that he'd installed. Dad was working on a short film for a Web site that had hired him as a consultant. He'd been doing all kinds of different jobs related to the Internet, including starting up his own Web business.

Madison liked watching Dad work at the computer. It inspired her. Maybe she'd learn how to make her own mini-movies and attach those to her files?

After watching Dad for a while, Madison glanced at the bottom corner of the computer screen. "Oh no! Is that the right time?" she asked aloud.

Dad nodded. "Yes, it is. Why? Do you have to go?" He looked disappointed.

Madison leaped up and grabbed her bag. "I'm supposed to meet everyone ten minutes ago!"

"It's pouring rain outside, young lady," Dad cautioned.

"I know, I know, I'll be fine," Madison said, trying to reassure him.

Dad handed her an umbrella at the door. "You're absolutely sure you're okay walking to the café in this weather?" he asked. "I can give you a lift."

Madison giggled. She gave Dad a kiss on the cheek.

"You're absolutely sure you're okay watching Phinnie?" she said.

"Aren't you the comedian?" Dad said. "Hey—don't forget to call me later. And you need to be back by five o'clock, okay? Stephanie's cooking dinner tonight. I want to spend some time with you! We want to talk to you about your summer plans. You need to make some!"

"Okay, okay!" Madison nodded, walking out quickly.

The streets were wet, but the air smelled warm and sticky like summer. Madison hurried along, umbrella overhead. Staying in downtown Far Hills was so much fun, she thought as she crossed a busy street. She was right here in the middle of everything.

Since it was raining, the cyber café and bookstore was packed with senior citizens, moms, dads, babies, and high-school kids. Aimee jumped out from behind the register the moment she saw Madison enter the store.

"You're here!" Aimee squealed, dashing over to the door.

Mr. Gillespie let out a loud, "Shhh!" He didn't want Aimee or her friends disturbing other customers.

"Hey," Madison said meekly. She shoved her umbrella into a stand by the store's front door and skipped over to a table in the back. Fiona was sitting there reading a copy of *Teen Scene* with a picture of pop star Nikki on the cover.

"What's up?" Fiona asked when she saw Madison.

"I have to get back to the front to help Dad, but you guys wait here. I get a break in ten minutes," Aimee said.

Madison watched Aimee go back to the front of the store. "Are you the only one here?" Madison asked Fiona.

Fiona shrugged. "No," she said, pointing into the "cyber" part of the store. "My brother's here, and so is Egg." She smiled. "And the other guys, too."

Fiona's twin brother, Chet, was seated around a computer monitor with Egg, Hart, and Drew Maxwell, all friends from school. They were laughing at something on the screen. Madison's eye caught Hart's, and he nudged the other guys. They started to walk over.

"Hey, Maddie!" Egg called out, slapping her on the back the way he always did. Sometimes Madison was sure that Egg forgot she was a girl. He treated her like one of the guys half the time.

"Hey, Finnster," Hart said, sitting down.

Madison sat between him and Drew. Egg and Chet took seats on the other side of the table next to Fiona.

"This stinks." Egg groaned. "We had swim lessons in the rain this morning, but I wanted it to be sunny. I need to get a tan. I need to keep my glow," he complained.

Madison snickered. "Yeah, getting a tan is a good reason to be a lifeguard."

"At least I'm doing something for the summer," Egg teased.

Madison pursed her lips like she was about to say something nasty in response, but she said nothing.

"How's the house painting going?" Hart asked Chet.

"Dad is bugging me because it's a Victorian, so it needs all these different colors. At least he's paying me to do it," Chet said. "Until I go to camp."

"That's so cool," Hart said.

"You never said your dad was paying you," Egg wailed.

Chet nodded. "At least I'm not living in the library like my sister."

Fiona punched him. "Shut up!" she said. "What's wrong with the book-a-thon? Reading is good for you. And the prize is two hundred dollars. That's like getting paid. Besides, you don't even read books!"

"I do so read books!" Chet yelled. He broke up. "I read the manual for my Robo-Bug computer game."

All the guys laughed.

"So all three of you started lifeguarding?" Madison spontaneously asked Egg, Drew, and Hart at the same time. "How is it?"

Drew answered first. "Yeah, we're learning how to give mouth-to-mouth resuscitation and all that," he explained. "The American Red Cross teaches it. We practice on rubber people. Started today. It's funny."

"Nah. It's dumb," Egg said.

"It saves lives," Hart said seriously.

Egg made a face. "Are you kidding me?"

Madison wondered what it would be like to practice mouth-to-mouth on a real person—like Hart. Was it like real kissing? She turned away so she wouldn't stare at Hart's lips.

"Hey, Egg, we have the most important job at the pool," Hart said.

"Come on!" Egg said. "We're junior lifeguards. We're not actually saving anyone. This isn't *Baywatch*, for Pete's sake."

"You shouldn't really joke about saving lives," Fiona said aloud.

The table fell silent.

"What do you—" Egg started to say, but cut himself off. "Yeah, well . . . I guess you're right. Sorry, Fiona."

The other boys snickered. Before liking Fiona, Egg never apologized for saying stupid stuff. But now . . .

Madison liked it when the "new and improved" Egg appeared.

"So what did you say you're doing for the summer?" Drew asked Madison. "I forgot."

She put her finger up to her chin like she was in a serious thinker pose. "I could do almost anything . . ." Madison started to say.

"You can still do the book-a-thon with me," Fiona said.

"Nah," Madison said. "You keep saying that, but I told you I don't want to."

"Aren't you volunteering at the animal clinic?" Egg asked. "You always do that. You and Dan."

Madison rolled her eyes. She was friends with Dan, but the way Egg said that it sounded like she was *more* than friends.

"I'm not working at the clinic. I'm not spending the summer with Dan," Madison said quickly. She looked over at Hart. "Actually, I was thinking of just hanging by the pool for a while."

Hart smiled. "And if you fall in the water, we'll save you," he said.

Madison smiled back.

It was a definite moment.

Of course, all good moments must come to an end. Madison's moment ended three seconds later. Aimee bounded over from the front counter.

"Hiya, everyone! Didja miss me? Have you guys decided what we should do this afternoon?"

"It's still pouring rain out," Drew said. "I say we should go to the movies."

"I can't," Chet said. "Dad wants us back home by four."

"Really?" Egg said, looking over at Fiona. "Bummer."

"We have to help our parents cook for this church potluck supper thing," Fiona explained.

"I can go to the movies," Hart said. "Who else can go?"

He looked right at Madison.

Be home by five. She could hear Dad's voice inside her head.

"I have to go home, too," Madison said. "Double bummer."

Drew, Egg, and Hart decided to brave the rain and walk over to the Far Hills triplex alone. Aimee got behind the bookstore counter again.

Disappointed, Madison and Fiona packed up their stuff and headed for the door.

In the doorway of Mr. Gillespie's cyber café, he'd posted an enormous bulletin board with the words COMMUNITY CHEST on top. The board was covered in colored file cards with all different kinds of messages and handwriting. People advertised futons, free kittens, and ten ways to make more money at home. There was even a book readers' classified section of the bulletin board, where people posted their favorite reads in order to get matched up for a date.

Madison didn't usually read the messages, but today she stopped and glanced at the rainbow of file cards. Fiona looked over the board, too.

"Hey, Maddie," Fiona said. "Did you see this? You have to read this one."

Madison looked under the bulletin board section marked JUST POSTED. Fiona pointed to a crisp pink file card with neat lettering on it.

> **Wanted: Mother's Helper for 2½-year-old boy.**
> Need someone during the week and some Saturdays to play with my son while I am with my newborn baby girl. Duties: feed lunch, play games, take to Lake Dora pool, and other activities. A parent will always be around to help you. We have 2 cats and live in a safe area near Blueberry Street. Some experience is a plus.
> Must be at least 12 years old.
> Call Mrs. Sandra Reed anytime. 555-1010

"Maddie, this is so perfect for you!" Fiona said.

"But I don't have any experience," Madison said. "How am I supposed to baby-sit? I don't know. It sounds hard."

Fiona plucked the card off the board. "Here, you should call her. It's right down the street from your house! Baby-sitting can be hard—but it can also be a lot of fun. Oh, it'll be so easy. You'll get paid for going to the pool. And she has cats! What's better than that?"

Madison's head was spinning.

Was this the big summer opportunity she'd been waiting for?

She folded the card and stuffed it into the pocket of her shorts before heading back to Dad's apartment in the warm rain.

Chapter 3

"Hello? Is this Mrs. Reed?" Madison's voice quivered as she spoke into the receiver. She clutched the pink file card in her hand.

"Hello?" a woman answered on the other end of the line. Her voice was soft and deep. "May I help you?"

"I'm calling about the card on the cyber café board," Madison explained. "About the baby-sitting . . . er . . . mother's helper job."

"Oh," Mrs. Reed said. "That's terrific! What's your name?"

"Madison Finn," she answered. "I'm twelve."

"Very good. Have you ever baby-sat before?"

Madison paused and took a breath. "Um . . . not

really. I pet sit sometimes. I volunteer down at the animal clinic. Does that count?"

Mrs. Reed laughed. "Well, now, pets and kids aren't exactly the same . . . but that's okay. Experience isn't entirely necessary. I'd like to give someone a chance to get experience. This won't be a hard job at all."

"Oh?" Madison said, sounding more intrigued than ever. "What does the job involve . . . exactly?"

"Well, playtime, really," Mrs. Reed explained. "Going to the Lake Dora pool, taking Eliot to activities. It depends. It will be fun."

Madison could feel her pulse race. *It actually sounded fun.*

"Tell me a little more about yourself," Mrs. Reed asked. "Do you have brothers and sisters?"

Madison explained that she was an only child. She told Mrs. Reed all about Phinnie and her laptop computer and her mom, the film producer. Mrs. Reed seemed very happy to "meet Madison by phone."

"I'd like to meet you in person," Mrs. Reed suggested. "And I'll need to speak to your mom or dad, too. Can we arrange that?"

Madison felt her hands shaking a little. She was nervous. Mrs. Reed made everything sound so official right away—like a real job.

"Okay, that's fine," Madison said. "I'm sure I can meet you soon. . . ."

"How about tomorrow morning?" Mrs. Reed asked.

"Well, I can ask my dad. . . ."

"Good! Do that!" Mrs. Reed said. "I'll wait for you two to call me back. Okay? Madison?"

This was all moving so fast, Madison couldn't believe it.

"Okay," she answered with a gulp.

"I have a feeling this may work out perfectly," Mrs. Reed said as Madison said good-bye.

"Thanks," Madison replied. "I hope it does work out. Perfectly."

When Madison put down the receiver, she jumped into the air like an acrobat and clicked her heels together.

"I got a jooooobbb!" she cried, running into the dining room. Dad and Stephanie were setting the table for dinner.

"What did you say?" Dad asked.

"I did it, Dad! You are now looking at the possible baby-sitter for the summer!"

"That's great," Stephanie said. "Congratulations, Maddie."

"All I need is for Dad to talk to Mrs. Reed—she's the woman with the baby. Mrs. Reed says she needs to make sure that you say it's okay, since I'm twelve. She wants to make sure I'm a good person for the job."

Madison was talking faster than fast.

"Of course!" Dad said. "Isn't that how these things usually work?" He looked over at Stephanie for reassurance.

"I'm sure you have a few questions, Jeff," Stephanie said matter-of-factly. "Let's call Mrs. Reed after we finish eating."

Dad grinned. "Maddie, I am so proud of you." He leaned over and lifted Madison right up off her feet. "To think that I was giving you such a hard time about finding something to do this summer," he gushed. "I only wanted you to get out of the house so you wouldn't be stuck inside all day. But a job—with responsibilities—that's impressive."

Stephanie's taco dinner was deliciously spicy, but all Madison could think about was baby-sitting. Her stomach flip-flopped. She could barely make dinner conversation. It was a big deal—especially since she'd only just dodged the summer job question with her friends that afternoon. All Madison wanted to do was tell Aimee and Fiona and Mom and everyone else who mattered . . . NOW.

Immediately following the meal, she bolted into her room to go online—and left Dad to call Mrs. Reed.

The moment she logged on to her laptop, Madison found her keypal Bigwheels online, too.

That was a very good omen.

```
<MadFinn>: Surprise! Ur online???
```

29

\<Bigwheels\>: This never happens to
    us!
\<MadFinn\>: I know & I thought u
    were @ horse camp
\<Bigwheels\>: not for a week next
    Monday
\<MadFinn\>: HUGE NEWS I MIGHT GET A
    JOB
\<Bigwheels\>: RUKM?
\<MadFinn\>: nope I wanna be a
    babyspitter
\<Bigwheels\>: Huh?
\<MadFinn\>: I mean SITTER! I am so
    excited I can't spell LOL
\<Bigwheels\>: that is great. Have u
    ever done it b4
\<MadFinn\>: nope but the mother says
    that's ok
\<Bigwheels\>: how old is the kid?
\<MadFinn\>: 2 and a half yrs old a
    boy his name's Eliot isn't that
    cute like the kid in ET
\<Bigwheels\>: I baby-sit sometimes
    for my cousin when his mom goes
    to the supermarket and stuff.
\<MadFinn\>: is it hard?
\<Bigwheels\>: haven't u ever read The
    Babysitters Club?
\<MadFinn\>: Yeah but that book's not
    real life
\<Bigwheels\>: they have a lot of

30

```
good ideas though & I have this
book of baby-sitting tips 2
<MadFinn>: u do? Then u totally
have 2 give me advice—as usual u
r the greatest keypal ever
<Bigwheels>: no prob!! The mom will
be there w/u right?
<MadFinn>: OC hey—what do I wear to
meet the kid 4 the first time?
<Bigwheels>: nice shorts and a
pretty shirt and wear sneakers
then it looks like ur ready
to go play
```

"Maddie!" Dad's voice echoed through the apartment. "I just got off the telephone. . . ."

Madison looked up from the computer monitor. Mrs. Reed and Dad had finished talking—*already*?

"I'll be right there, Dad!" Madison called out. She typed another message to Bigwheels at the same time.

```
<MadFinn>: have 2 go now :>(
<Bigwheels>: GL at ur interview
<MadFinn>: thanks I need it
<Bigwheels>: TMA—you'll be FAB!
<MadFinn>: CWYL
<Bigwheels>: *poof*
```

"That Mrs. Reed is a nice woman . . ." Dad said as he strolled into Madison's room, "I think I know her husband—oh, honey, I didn't realize you were online."

"I'm not anymore," Madison said. She clicked the sleep function key and her screen went black. "Dad, tell me. What did you say? What did *she* say? Did she ask you questions about me?"

Dad sat on the edge of Madison's bed. "We had a very nice chat. I think that you made a good job choice. Her son, Eliot, sounds like a good kid. He's been struggling a little bit since his sister was born."

"Struggling?" Madison asked.

"Yeah, it's hard when there's a new baby in the family. She wants him to get the right amount of attention this summer. That's why she needs a helper," Dad said. "I told her it sounded like the perfect job for you."

"So what do I do now?" Madison said. Her knee was bouncing up and down. Her arms flapped like wings. Madison couldn't keep any body parts still.

"Maddie." Dad laughed. "Just relax. I'll drive you over there in the morning and you can meet. I'm sure she's going to offer you the position. She sounded enthusiastic. She just wants to see how you and Eliot get along in person."

Madison's skin felt all hot like it did when she ran too fast or when she bumped into Hart in the hallway at school. She was about to get her first job. She had to remember to breathe.

"What if Eliot doesn't like me?" Madison asked.

Dad shook his head. "That's impossible," he said in a booming voice.

The morning ride over to Mrs. Reed's house took forever. Madison plucked at the seat belt pulled across her chest and kicked at the car floor mat. On the way to the Reed house, she and Dad drove past Madison's house on Blueberry Street, which seemed weird. As much as she loved staying at Dad's, she missed her room and the half-full closet of clothes she'd left behind.

Madison turned so she could see the front porch, wishing she were there right now.

"This must be the place," Dad said as he pulled into a driveway around the corner.

It was the house Madison had guessed it would be. Mrs. Reed lived in a brick, two-story house with rows of black-eyed Susans along her fence. Madison and Phin *had* passed it on their daily walks before.

Dad walked Madison up to the door and rang the bell. When Mrs. Reed opened it, he reached out to shake her hand, but her arms were full. She was holding her newborn baby girl.

"Hello!" Mrs. Reed said. "You must be Madison Finn!" She juggled the baby girl into one arm and reached out to shake with the free hand.

"She's so cute," Madison said softly.

The baby cooed.

"This is Becka," Mrs. Reed introduced her. She opened the door wider and invited Madison and her father inside. "Please have a seat. I know Eliot will be right down."

Dad and Madison went into the living room. There were colored plastic toy trucks and trains piled at the side of the room. Madison and her dad took a seat on a long leather couch.

Mrs. Reed called upstairs. "Eliot! Eliot! We have guests! Come downstairs, please."

Madison squirmed in her seat. She couldn't wait to see her new friend. She hoped he wouldn't spit in her face or run screaming from the room as soon as he saw her sitting there.

Eliot loped down the stairs slowly, clinging to the banister rails. "What, Mama?"

"I'd like you to meet our new friend, Madison. She's going to be helping Mama this summer. Remember I told you that we would have a friend take you to the pool and play in the water?"

Eliot nodded. He jumped off the bottom step and ran right for his mother's left leg. He clung so hard his fingers left white marks on Mrs. Reed's sunburned skin.

"Okay, now, Eliot. I want you to say hello to Madison. Can you do that?" Mrs. Reed pushed him gently off her leg, and he let out a little scream.

Dad leaned over to Madison. "He's a cutie," Dad said. "He'll warm up to you in no time."

Eliot stared at Madison without moving. She was beginning to panic.

"Go ahead and say hello," Mrs. Reed said, encouraging him. "Why don't you show Madison your new blue truck?"

Madison searched the floor for the truck. She lifted it into the air. "Is this yours?" she asked aloud. "Should we play with it?"

Eliot stuck his thumb into his mouth and started to suck hard. He shook his head and murmured. "Mmmmmnnnnnn," he said. Madison didn't know if that was a yes or a no.

Becka let out a teeny squeal, and Eliot turned around to face his sister. He pointed at her. "My baby," he said. "My baby sistah."

Madison nodded. "She's nice. How old is your sister?" she asked.

Mrs. Reed smiled. "Eliot, why don't you show Madison your train set in the other room?"

Eliot shook his head. "No," he said.

Madison blinked. "Oh, well," she joked. "We can do something else."

Eliot smiled. "Pee-pee," he said.

Madison's face blanched white for a second. "Huh? Um . . . is that some kind of game?" she asked Mrs. Reed.

Mrs. Reed chuckled softly. "No, Madison. He has to go to the bathroom. We're just starting potty training. He still wears diapers sometimes, but he's doing better."

"Pee-pee! Pee-pee!" Eliot yelled. He stomped his feet and jumped up and down a little without ever taking his chewed-on thumb out of his mouth.

Mrs. Reed called him over and gently whispered in his ear. Eliot disappeared into the next room, and Madison was sure he was off to the bathroom. But he came right back with a wooden train car that was painted red and black. Mrs. Reed made a little face at him, and he vanished again—this time for the bathroom.

Madison tapped her feet, crossed and then uncrossed her arms. She was still feeling a little nervous.

"Eliot seems like a great kid," Dad said to Mrs. Reed. "He's very cute."

She nodded. "He's just having a hard time with his new sister. But I suspect it won't last. Especially once he becomes your friend, Madison!"

Madison raised her eyebrows. "So does that mean I have the job?" she asked.

"I hope so!" Mrs. Reed said. "We would all love to have you!"

Dad put his arm around Madison's shoulders and squeezed.

"When can you start?" Mrs. Reed asked.

"Whenever you need me," Madison said with a shrug. "Tomorrow?"

"Hooray!" Mrs. Reed said. "Tomorrow it is."

Even little Becka cooed.

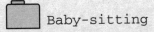 Baby-sitting

Rude Awakening: The joke's on me—I'm going to be kidding around all summer long. Well, taking care of ONE kid, anyway.

But I am so-o-o psyched. Mrs. Reed is excellent. Plus she makes great lemonade that I will drink every day now.

Dad and I stayed over at her house for almost an hour this morning. The time went by so fast. And Eliot seemed kind of shy, but he showed me his train car eventually— that is, when he finally let go of his mom's leg. And their two cats, Peanut Butter and Jelly, were friendly most of the time, until Jelly hissed at me and ran under the couch. But who cares about that.

This is a monumental day. I can't
believe I have my first real job!!! I am a
real baby-sitter!!!

The really, REALLY cool part is that I
will be getting paid $5 an hour for about
five hours a day. That is, like, $125 a
week, and that is so much money. Now who's
slacking off this summer, Egg? LOL. I can't
wait to start. I am still a little nervous
about doing something I've never done
before, but how hard can baby-sitting
really be? I mean, hanging out, playing,
and swimming . . . what's so tough about that?

**Madison hit SAVE and opened a new e-mail
just for her keypal. She marked it with a priority
exclamation point, of course.**

From: MadFinn
To: Bigwheels
Subject: Wish You Were Here
Date: Thurs 19 June 12:46 PM

Guess what? I GOT THE JOB!!! And
it's all thanks to you. So now I
have like a zillion questions about
what games I should play and what
else I can do when I actually DO
start (which is tomorrow), but right
now I have to go to meet my friends
at the pool TA-DA!

Is ur little sister away @ camp

right now? Oh, BTW, I forgot to
mention that Hart will be at the
pool all summer

(((((:-{=

Yours till the baby sits,

Maddie

p.s. What r u doing reading this? u
should be outside in the SUN! LOL.

After hitting SEND and checking her e-mailbox
one last time for any last-minute messages, Madison
logged off. She had to hurry! Everyone would be
waiting for her at the pool by Lake Dora. And she
hadn't even picked out what bathing suit she wanted
to wear.

*What kind of bathing suit would a baby-sitter
wear?*

Madison's brain whizzed. Within the span of a
few hours, *everything* had changed.

"Hey, Phinnie," Madison called out to her dog.
"Should I wear the turquoise bandeau with the terry
cloth shorts or my tube top and the red shorts?"

Phin snorted. He was busy chewing on a fake rubber newspaper called *The Doggy Dog Times.*

"These make my legs look weird," Madison said,
holding the shorts up to her reflection in the mirror. "And
I can't really wear this top because I have no boobs."

Madison sighed and finally decided on a light-yellow cropped T-shirt with a sun drawn on the middle of it and a pair of Hawaiian-style shorts. She got dressed quickly, slipping on her two-piece bathing suit under the shirt and shorts. Afterward Madison punched up the computer screen once again. She needed to see her calendar for the summer.

As of today, she had very important things to add. Madison cross-referenced important dates with the Lake Dora pool schedule that she'd taken from the recreation center director's office.

LAKE DORA CLUBHOUSE SUMMER

Outdoor season begins June 14 and ends in mid-September. Contact pro office for details on becoming a member.

SWIMMING

Lake Dora has two pools and a series of swimming docks. Main pool and lake docks are open all day until dusk. Qualified swimmers age 7 and up may swim without a parent. All other children must be accompanied by a parent or guardian. No exceptions.

Madison smiled to herself. That's what she was now. A *guardian*. She read the rest of the flyer.

TENNIS

Lake Dora has four asphalt and two clay courts. Open to members only. Lessons available. Contact clubhouse manager or tennis pro, Ed Wicks.

ACTIVITIES

Please see daily blackboard for children's activities, including pool games, volleyball, horseshoes, family kickball, and assorted theme weeks. Summer kicks off with the POOL DAY competition in swimming and racing. Assistant lifeguard programs available for children age 12 and up. Summer positions available: pool cleanup, snack shop assistant, and junior game master. Hurry! Classes fill quickly.

EVENINGS

Junior party area is open on Friday and Saturday evenings. You must be at least 12 to attend any of the junior barbecues or dances. The following are planned for summer: Italian Night (pizza party), Halloween Night (costumes and candy bingo), South of the Border Night (piñatas and tacos), and Magic Show (prizes to be awarded).

There was too much to do! Madison wondered how she could have started out the summer without a clue. Now she had a mile-long list of plans!

"Maddie!" Dad's voice called out. "I know you're working on the laptop, but I think we better take off. It'll be sundown before you even get to the pool."

Dad was exaggerating. It was only one o'clock.

Madison quickly checked her reflection to make sure that the shorts fit okay and that her bathing suit straps weren't showing. Phin rubbed up against her leg as if to say, "Don't go to the pool! Stay here and snuggle with me!" but Madison promptly gave him the brush-off.

"Phinnie," she said gently. "Stephanie is going to take you for a walk this afternoon, okay? I'll be back later." She kissed the top of his head, and he let out a long, hot sigh.

"Dad! I'm coming!" Madison squealed, tossing her pool flip-flops into her bag and dashing to the door. She couldn't wait to see Hart in his swim trunks and shades. She knew he'd look cuter than cute, even with sunblock smeared all over his nose.

In the car on the way over, Dad talked more about Mrs. Reed and the baby-sitting job. "You know, Maddie," Dad said, "I am so proud of you. And your mom is going to be proud, too."

Madison wished she could have shared the job news with Mom in person.

"But having a job will make the summer very different," Dad continued. "I'll bet this afternoon is the last day for a while that you get to hang out at Lake Dora with just your friends."

"What do you mean?" Madison asked.

Dad shrugged. "Well, you have little Eliot to take care of now."

"What does Eliot have to do with my friends?" Madison asked. She gazed out the window as they drove.

As Dad pulled into the Lake Dora parking lot, Madison spotted Fiona and Aimee standing over by the snack shop. She hopped out of the car, gave Dad a quick kiss, and hurried away.

"Maddie!" Aimee and Fiona screeched at the same time.

Madison waved. "You both look awesome—as usual."

Fiona giggled.

"So?" Aimee said expectantly.

"So?" Madison repeated.

"Tell us how it went!" Aimee blurted. "Did you get the job? Did you meet the woman from the ad? What happened?"

Madison grinned. "Oh yeah. She gave me the job."

Eeeeeeeeeeeeeeeeek!

All three girls squealed.

"Whoa, Maddie," Fiona said. "That is so great!"

Aimee gave Madison a big squeeze. "We said you would get it!"

"I can't believe it," Madison said. "Now I have real plans, just like you."

"Hey, Finnster!"

Madison felt her body straighten up as soon as she heard Hart's voice. He waved to all three girls as he walked past on his way to the lifeguard area. Egg and Drew were already inside.

"Hart's a nice guy," Aimee said, twirling her blond hair. "If he wasn't going out with Ivy Daly, I think I might like him."

Fiona giggled again. "Then you and Hart and Egg and I could double-date."

43

"Yeah, and Maddie could go with Dan or Drew and we could triple-date!" Aimee added.

Madison's jaw dropped. Sometimes her BFFs said the strangest things. Madison didn't even know how to respond, so she just ignored the comments. They didn't *mean* anything. Aimee had no real interest in pursuing Hart because she was too much in like with Ben Buckley, right? And any stories of Hart and Ivy were just unconfirmed junior-high rumors, right? Madison certainly wasn't planning any kind of dates with Dan or Drew, right?

Good grief.

The girls went into the pool area together and dropped their towels and bags onto the nearest chairs. Aimee flipped on sunglasses and tried to pretend that her brother Dean and his friends weren't sitting four chairs away.

"I miss ballet," Aimee said wistfully. "The classes stopped for a couple of weeks before summer sessions."

"Go swimming instead," Madison suggested.

"The only problem is that I don't want to get wet and mess up my hair." Aimee sighed.

"Are you kidding?" Madison asked. "You don't want to get wet?"

Fiona snorted.

"Well, no," Aimee said. "I don't want to get wet."

Aimee pulled on a straw hat and her Discman headphones and applied Tan-a-rama lotion to her legs and arms. Of course, Madison knew that behind her shades, Aimee was searching the pool crowd for Ben Buckley.

"Has anyone seen Egg?" Fiona asked. Now that they were an "item," Fiona always seemed to have Egg on the brain.

"He's over there," Madison said, pointing across to a crowd of kids. He was standing with Drew and Hart, and they were all wearing the same green swim trunks and white muscle shirt, the "official" pool uniform. Since they were working, the boys couldn't come over to chat. They waved from a safe distance.

Fiona waved back. Then she pulled out one of her library book-a-thon books and settled back into the pool chair.

Madison had rushed out of Dad's without bringing anything to read or listen to. She looked over at Aimee and then Fiona and then back at Aimee again like she was watching a silent tennis match.

"Um, excuse me?" Madison asked aloud. "Are you just going to read?"

"Yeah." Fiona smiled. "I thought we were just hanging out," she said.

"Sure," Madison said. "But aren't we going to talk or something? I mean, Aimee's got her music on, you're reading—what am I supposed to do?"

Fiona shrugged. "Maddie, what's the biggie? We have all summer to talk."

Madison nodded. "Of course," she said. "All summer."

But then a part of her thought about what Dad said.

I'll bet this afternoon is the last day for a while that you get to hang out at Lake Dora with just your friends.

What if Dad was right?

"Hey, you guys," Aimee whispered, pulling off her headphones. "Look who's over there. . . ."

Fiona and Madison glanced up to see Ivy Daly and her drones making their entrance into the pool area. Ivy was wearing a bikini and the shortest shorts Madison had ever seen, with a patch on the back that said SWEET.

"She never looks fat." Aimee sighed.

"That's because she's perfect," Madison said jokingly.

"Maddie, when do you have to start baby-sitting?" Fiona asked.

"Tomorrow," Madison replied. "But the cool part is that I think I'll be coming here to the pool with Eliot and his mom. So I can hang out with you just like we're doing now."

"That is cool," Fiona said. "We have to stick together this summer even if we are going out with guys."

"Fiona, you're the only one going out with anyone," Aimee reminded her.

A voice over the Lake Dora loudspeaker boomed.

"YOUR ATTENTION, PLEASE. FREE SWIM HAS ENDED. KIDDIE POOL IS CLOSED UNTIL THREE

46

O'CLOCK. SIGN-UPS FOR POOL DAY IN THE MAIN LODGE. THANK YOU."

"Oh yeah! I have to sign up for Pool Day," Fiona said. "I bet my brother that I could beat him at one of the swimming races."

"I am totally doing the races, too," Madison said. "I've been looking forward to this since last summer. How about you, Aimee?"

"Nah, I'll be your cheerleader," Aimee said from behind her sunglasses. "I told you . . ."

"You don't want to get wet?" Madison laughed.

Madison knew the real reason. Aimee was a nervous swimmer. Ever since they'd been little girls, she'd been afraid of the deep end of the pool. When Aimee was five, she'd fallen into the water and stayed under for almost a minute. She'd had the wind knocked out of her and swallowed a pint of pool water. One of the pool lifeguards had to give her CPR to get her breathing again.

"Do you guys want to go to the snack shop?" Fiona asked. It was located closer to the junior lifeguard station.

"OH, MY GOODNESS!" Aimee said loudly. She clapped her hands over her mouth. "He's here," she whispered.

"Who?" Madison asked. She turned around to see Ben Buckley entering the pool area with his older sister and little brother. He was carrying a giant bag and towels.

"His family has one of the cabanas," Aimee whispered.

The Lake Dora pool offered private cabanas for families who paid extra membership dues. It also had a special recreation room, a video game arcade area, tennis courts, and even a small archery range.

But Ben walked past without even saying hello to Aimee.

She sank back into her chair.

"Didn't he see you?" Fiona asked.

"You're wearing a hat," Madison said. "Maybe he didn't recognize you."

"Whatever," Aimee said, her eyes still following him.

Madison scanned the lifeguard area for another glimpse of Hart. He wasn't in view, but Madison did catch sight of a small boy with a shock of red hair spiking every which way on top of his head. The little boy was running—screaming—to a woman Madison guessed was his baby-sitter.

For a brief moment, Madison forgot all about Hart.

She began to think about the *new* guy in her life. Eliot Reed.

Chapter 5

Madison stood outside the door of the Reed house, bouncing on her toes.

Their doorbell sounded like chimes. The bristly mat outside the front door said WELCOME TO OUR HOME. Rows of purple, pink, and red petunias decorated the front lawn. A large white flowering bush near the front steps smelled like mom's perfume.

Madison liked everything about the Reed house so far.

Dad had driven Madison to her new job this morning from downtown Far Hills. His place was convenient—only ten minutes away. But Madison couldn't wait until Mom returned and she went back to living in their normal house. Then Madison would be able to walk to Mrs. Reed's place in less than five minutes. *That* was convenient.

No one answered the Reeds' bell right away. Madison pressed it again.

All at once, the big wooden door flew wide open. Eliot stood there, both hands on the doorknob. He scrunched up his nose and glared at Madison.

She cracked a bright smile and started to move inside, but then, *SLAM!*

The door shut in her face.

She knocked lightly. "Eliot? It's Maddie. Do you remember me? Eliot? Could you get your mommy?"

Madison rang the bell again so his mom would hear it.

Once again the door flew open and Eliot was there. He scowled this time, but didn't slam. Madison reached out so the door wouldn't close in her face.

"Madison!" Mrs. Reed called. She was huffing, out of breath. "I was upstairs putting Becka back down for a little morning nap. She's always extra sleepy in the mornings after her bottle. How are you?"

Madison shrugged. "Fine," she said.

Eliot grabbed his mom's leg.

"I'm excited to be here," Madison said. "Should I come inside?"

"Of course you should come in!" Mrs. Reed said, chuckling. She shooed Eliot off her leg while she guided Madison into the living room. "Have a seat, sweetie," Mrs. Reed said.

Eliot lunged for his mother again as she sat on the sofa. Unfortunately, he landed on the floor.

He started to cry immediately.

"Oh, Eliot," Mrs. Reed said. "Come here." She lifted him into her lap, and he popped his thumb into his mouth. "As you can see," Mrs. Reed explained, "he's excited, too. It'll probably take him a little while to get used to you."

Madison didn't mind. She gazed at his blue eyes, lost in his nervous stare. "How are you, Eliot?" Madison asked.

Eliot just kept staring.

"I thought that today we could spend part of this morning here. I can give you a tour of the house and show you where things are. Then later this afternoon we can go over to Lake Dora for a swim at the pool," Mrs. Reed said.

"Thwim!" Eliot cried. He sucked hard on his thumb. "Thwim! Thwim! Thwim!"

"Eliot loves the water," Mrs. Reed said. "As I'm sure you guessed."

"Some friends of mine are actually junior life-guards there this summer," Madison said.

"Isn't that nice?" Mrs. Reed said. She unclipped a baby monitor from her side pocket and turned up

51

the volume. "I hope she stays down for a nice nap. She has been going through a real growth spurt lately. She's fussy all the time."

"Ussy! Ussy!" Eliot said.

"Now, Eliot, you don't talk like a baby, do you?" Mrs. Reed said. "I think that Madison deserves to hear you talk like a big boy."

Eliot stared. He said nothing. The thumb fell away from his mouth.

"Do you want to play with some toys?" Madison asked him.

Eliot shrugged. "Nope," he said. The thumb went back into the mouth.

"Don't mind him," Mrs. Reed said.

"Oh, I don't," Madison said. She didn't know if she was supposed to be doing something—anything—to distract Eliot.

Waaaaaaaaaaaaaaaaah!

A muffled cry crackled over the monitor.

Waaaaaaaaaaaaaaaaah!

"Drat!" Mrs. Reed said. "Let me go get Becka and change her diaper. Will you two be all right down here?"

Madison nodded.

Eliot let go of the thumb once again. "Mama!" he cried out.

Mrs. Reed pushed him away gently. "I'll be right back," she said.

Eliot started to wail.

"I'll be right back," Mrs. Reed said a second time. "I promise." She kissed Eliot on top of his head and handed him a toy truck.

He dove onto the floor and pushed it around on the carpet. Madison could see a little tear on his cheek.

"That's a supercool truck," Madison said.

"No!" Eliot grunted. "No! No! No!"

"No?" Madison asked. "Why not?"

"My tuck," Eliot said. "MY TUCK!"

"I know," Madison explained. She got down on the floor with Eliot. "Your truck is nice. . . . That's all I was saying. . . . I know it's *your* truck."

THWACK!

Eliot hit Madison on the shoulder with the truck and then ran into the next room. Madison winced in pain, but it lasted only a few moments.

"Eliot!" she called out. "Where are you going?"

"My tucks!" Eliot screamed. He pointed to a chest in the corner of the dining room. It was overflowing with trucks in all colors and shapes and sizes. In fact, the entire room was filled with toys overflowing out of boxes and crates and even a plastic laundry hamper in one corner.

"Wow," Madison said. "You have a lot of toys. I guess we won't be getting bored."

"Madison?" Mrs. Reed's voice cut through the air. "Are you in here?"

Madison told her they were looking at toys in the dining room.

As soon as Mrs. Reed walked in, Eliot took his trucks one by one and whipped them out of a crate and onto the floor. It made a huge noise that upset his little baby sister, Becka.

"Oh, Eliot!" Mrs. Reed cried, trying to calm down Becka.

Madison rushed over to the toy mess and scrambled to pick it up. "I'm sorry. I should have—"

"Nonsense!" Mrs. Reed said. "Eliot's just not used to having someone new around, right, honey?"

Eliot sniffled. "I wanna thwim."

"Maybe we should go now," Mrs. Reed said, turning to Madison. "Would you help me get the kids' stuff together? I can give you a tour of the house while we do that."

Madison got up off the floor and brushed off her knees. She hoped that once she and Eliot had spent a few days together, they'd become the best of friends. That was how it always worked out in books and movies.

The upstairs floor of the Reed house was covered in the kind of deep, plush, wall-to-wall carpet that made it easy to fall asleep lying down. Eliot loved rolling around on it, Madison noticed. He had little carpet fuzz all over his shirt.

Mrs. Reed pointed them toward the kids' rooms. Becka had a small nursery painted lemon yellow. She had a black-and-white mobile dangling over her bassinet and a motorized swing in the corner. Eliot opened up all of Becka's drawers to inspect their contents.

While Mrs. Reed changed Becka, she told Madison it would be tough to change Eliot's diapers. He was acting a little fussier lately.

Diapers? Madison had forgotten all about those.

"I told you yesterday he's trying to start potty training," Mrs. Reed explained. "But he hasn't quite figured it out. During the day, you can just keep a diaper on him and change it two or three times while you're here. Unless he tells you that he's gone to the—"

"POOOOOOOOP!" Eliot squealed with delight. It was obviously his favorite word.

Madison's stomach did a flip-flop.

Poop? She'd really forgotten all about that.

But Madison nodded "yes" and "okay" to everything Mrs. Reed said or asked. After all, she was used to walking Phinnie. She could get used to changing diapers. Hopefully.

Even though his mother had left the room, Eliot seemed calmer now. He had found his favorite blue dump truck and was loading and dumping magnetic alphabet letters onto the floor. He wasn't looking at Madison, but she didn't mind. She tried to play with him a little, and he stayed focused on his toys.

After about ten minutes, Mrs. Reed reappeared with two large tote bags crammed full. She handed one to Madison.

"Here, Madison," Mrs. Reed said sweetly. "Could you take Eliot's bag? Let's pack up the car."

Madison grabbed the bag and followed Mrs. Reed outside. Eliot ran ahead, but Mrs. Reed grabbed him by the waistband of his shorts. She buckled the kids into their car seats.

Eliot started fidgeting almost immediately. "I don't wanna! I don't wanna!" Eliot wailed.

Once again, Becka followed his lead. Within seconds the two were wailing in perfect harmony.

Madison tried to reach into the tote bag she was carrying to find some toy that would make Eliot smile and stop fussing. But when she reached in, she pulled out a handful of towel and then everything flew out of the bag. Eliot's stuff went flying.

"Hahahahaha." Eliot stopped wailing for a moment and giggled. He made a raspberry. "Pffffffffffffffffft!"

Madison shot him a look and smiled. But the moment her lips curled into a grin, Eliot's giggles turned into a low whine again.

"What's wrong, El?" Mrs. Reed called into the backseat. "Becka, stop crying."

"Should I do something?" Madison asked. She tensed up. "Eliot, it's okay," Madison said.

"Let's just get in the car," Mrs. Reed said. "They'll be fine once we get going."

Madison climbed into the front seat, directly in

front of Eliot's car seat. He promptly pinged one of his little minitrucks at her head.

"Eliot!" his mother screamed. "I said no throwing in the car."

Becka's cry sounded lower and hoarse now. Madison could see her face had turned beet red.

"They'll be fine," Mrs. Reed said, trying to smile. "As soon as we get to the pool, Eliot will—"

"Thwim! Thwim! Thwim!" Eliot cried out from the back, winging another truck at Madison's head.

She scooted down in the seat as Mrs. Reed hit the gas.

And they were off: the mother, the baby-sitter, the baby, and the little boy who had obviously made a decision not to be happy in Madison's presence.

Madison wondered if the whole summer would be like this.

She sucked in a breath of cool air-conditioning in the car and hoped for the best.

The pool was packed. Mrs. Reed had to park in a space that was miles from the entrance. Well, not really *miles*, but it felt that far to Madison. She was now carrying both tote bags while Mrs. Reed held on to Becka. Eliot raced ahead of everyone.

"Pool! Pool! I wanna thwim!" he said, jumping into the air.

"Eliot, I told you to be careful. Now, slow down.

There are cars driving around here. You have to hold Madison's hand," Mrs. Reed said.

Madison ran to catch up to him and grabbed his hand.

Soon they were inside the main entrance. Eliot tugged on Madison's khaki shorts. "Come on!" he said, ordering Madison to follow him.

Suddenly he wanted to be friends? Madison was confused.

"Why don't you and Eliot go into the pool area and wait for us," Mrs. Reed suggested. "I'll just register you as my guest, and then we can find a place to sit."

"Okay," Madison said. She scanned the room for familiar faces. Were Aimee and Fiona here today? They promised they'd come.

"Finnster! Hey!" Hart came up behind Madison. He was carrying a kickboard for the pool. "What's up? Are you here with Fiona and Aim?"

Madison shook her head. "No. Actually, I'm here for my job. I'm a mother's helper. This is Eliot."

Madison pointed down to Eliot, who had his thumb stuck right back in his mouth. He looked up at Hart suspiciously.

"Do you like to swim, little buddy?" Hart asked.

Eliot nodded. "Thwim."

"Well, I have to go check in. We have to clean up the pool area for some swim test later on," Hart said. "See ya."

"Yeah, later," Madison said, nodding. Her crush disappeared into the crowd of other swimmers and lifeguards and parents and toddlers running around like wild animals.

Eliot wanted to join them all.

"Madison!" Mrs. Reed came wobbling over with Becka. "Here's your registration card. This says that you're helping take care of my kids. Just in case there's any kind of emergency. You know."

By some miracle, the four of them found two empty chairs in the middle of all the chaos. The air smelled sweet, like a hundred tubes of coconut oil. Speakers played a surfing, summer song that could be heard faintly behind the shrieks of kids playing Marco Polo.

Mrs. Reed sat down and pulled out a tube of sunblock cream. She handed it to Madison.

"No!" Eliot shrieked when Madison tried to rub some onto his shoulders. He was slippery and wiggled right out of her grip.

"Why don't you two head over to the kiddie pool?" Mrs. Reed suggested.

Madison couldn't believe that her job today had been such nonstop action. Couldn't Eliot just sit and play nicely while she spent more time hanging out, talking to her friends?

Eliot was tugging at Madison's shorts again. "Wanna go to pool," he said assertively. "Come on."

Madison grabbed his wrist, and the two walked

over to the kiddie-pool area. The pool wasn't very deep, but it looked hazardous all the same. There were dozens of toddlers and moms and brothers and sisters, and everyone was splashing at the exact same time.

In other words, Madison thought, it was the one place on the planet she didn't want to be.

And into the pool they went.

Madison helped Eliot put on an inflatable water float that looked like a little horsey. He looked cute when he wasn't yelling at her.

They walked down to an area near the wading pool steps. Eliot and another little girl got into a mini-splash fight. Madison broke it up when the girl splashed her.

"Eliot, let's swim," Madison suggested. "The water's a little deeper over there." It was about three feet deep. Eliot kicked and dog-paddled his way over with Madison behind him. The horsey kept him afloat.

"This is fun," Eliot said when they'd been in the water a few minutes.

Madison laughed to herself. It was a lot of fun, she thought, apart from the noise, aggravation, heat, and wet.

And Eliot was enjoying himself. He'd stopped fussing at last.

Soon they got a little tired and went back into the shallower part. Eliot took off his inflatable horsey and picked up a plastic boat he wanted to try out. They launched it from the side of the wading pool. By now some people had left the water, so there was more room to play. Madison began to enjoy Eliot—and her job. She also wanted to make sure Eliot stayed safe.

"Hey, let's put horsey back on," Madison suggested, fastening it around his body again. Eliot dunked himself and his boat into the pool and laughed.

"Giddyap, horsey!" he said.

From across the pool, Madison saw Egg and Drew strutting around the pool area, arms overflowing with towels. They had laundry duty today. Egg saw Madison looking and stuck out his tongue. She stuck hers out, too.

Splash!

Madison turned back around again to see what Eliot was doing. But he wasn't in the water anymore. He had jumped up onto the main pool deck and glanced back as if to say, "Wheee! I'm free!"

"Eliot!" Madison yelled. "What are you doing? Come back here, Eliot."

"No!" he yelled, laughing. He started to skip away. "No, no, no!"

"STOP THAT KID!" Madison yelled.

She nearly landed flat on her face as she jumped out of the pool after him.

Chapter 6

"I don't THINK so!" Hart said as he grabbed Eliot and held him close.

Madison scampered over to where Hart and Eliot stood, a few yards from the kiddie pool.

"Oh—thanks—Hart—Eliot—why?" Madison was breathless.

Hart smiled. "This little guy's fast."

"Fast!" Eliot repeated. "FAST!"

Madison quickly looked around to see if Mrs. Reed had seen what happened. She was over by the snack shop, holding Becka and chatting with another mom.

Whew.

Madison wiped her brow dramatically and tried

grabbing Eliot's hand, but he started to wiggle away again.

Hart leaned down and grabbed Eliot's plastic horsey. Hart reeled him in.

"So you want the tickle monster, huh?" Hart said to Eliot. "Well, that's what you'll get, then!"

Eliot looked like he might cry, and Madison prepared herself for the worst. But when Hart tickled him behind his knees and by his armpits, he began to squeal with delight.

"Stop! Stop! Ahhh!" Eliot was laughing so hard that his nose started running.

"Now you *laugh*?" Madison moaned. She told Hart about the morning's experiences. "Hey, Eliot, why don't you laugh for me?" Madison said playfully.

Of course, she was only half kidding.

Why *hadn't* he laughed for her?

Egg and Drew walked over. Their arms were still filled with towels.

"Excuse me, who said you could lounge around while we do all the work?" Egg said. "And who's this, Maddie? Your new boyfriend?"

Drew snorted a laugh. "He's the junior, junior lifeguard."

"Ha-ha-ha," Madison said. "Very funny, you guys."

Eliot was still wriggling. Madison took his hand in hers. "Let's go find your mommy," she whispered. "We can play a game with Becka, okay?"

"Mama." Eliot nodded.

Madison grabbed a dry towel from Egg and Drew and quickly led Eliot away from the boys, who were cracking jokes.

"Mama," Eliot said again. "Go see Mama!"

Whew.

He sounded happy. Madison was relieved. She took off the inflatable horse and headed over toward the snack shop and Mrs. Reed.

"Ooh, is someone getting a sunburn?" Mrs. Reed said when Madison approached. Becka was asleep in her stroller.

Madison shook her head. She was worried.

"I—I put on the waterproof sunblock, Mrs. Reed," Madison stammered. "Should I put on more? I'm so sorry—"

"Madison, don't worry," Mrs. Reed said, taking Eliot into her arms. He nuzzled his mom's neck. "Are you having fun with Madison, sweetie?"

Madison waited for Eliot to scream, "NOOOOOOOOO! I hate her!" but he didn't. He was sucking his thumb and asking for ice cream.

The rest of the afternoon was surprisingly uneventful. Madison lingered close while Eliot played with some of his toys in the shade. They ate snow cones together. Things were much easier when the four of them were all together.

Sometime after three o'clock a tall man walked up to Mrs. Reed. With his suit and dark glasses, he looked like a secret service agent, Madison thought. The man threw open his arms, and Eliot dove in for a giant hug.

"Daddeeeeeeee!" Eliot cried.

"Hey, big shot," Mr. Reed said. He leaned over and gave his wife and daughter a kiss. "So you must be Madison Finn?" he asked.

Madison smiled and extended her hand. "Yes," she said meekly. "Nice to meet you, Mr. Reed. Thanks for giving me this summer job."

Mr. Reed winked. Up close he looked like an important movie actor.

After chatting about swimming and suntans and Eliot's afternoon by the pool, the Reeds and Madison packed up the two tote bags. It was time to go.

Madison had survived—barely survived—her first day as a mother's helper. She looked around the pool one last time to see if Aimee or Fiona would magically appear, but neither BFF was there. Even Hart, Egg, and Drew were missing. "Oh, well," Madison told herself. "I guess I'll see them tomorrow."

"Thank you so much, Madison," Mrs. Reed said, grabbing Madison's hand and shaking it. It seemed like a weird thing to do, but Madison shook right back.

"Eliot, what do you say to Madison?" Mr. Reed said.

"I want a piggyback, Daddy," Eliot said. He looked up at the sky.

"Eliot," his father said again. "Don't you have something to tell Madison?"

Madison leaned down close to Eliot's face. "See ya tomorrow," she said. "We can play trucks again."

Eliot looked down at his feet. "Tucks," he said simply. Then he turned around to his dad. "Up, Daddy, up."

Madison shrugged. "I'll see you at the same time tomorrow," she said, smiling.

Mrs. Reed smiled back. "See you then."

Dad was standing in the doorway of Madison's room in his apartment, drumming his fingers against the door frame. "So, tell me what else happened on your first day, working girl. You haven't said much since I picked you up."

"Oh, Dad," Madison said, covering her face in mock embarrassment. "I told you."

"You haven't told me anything!" Dad said. "Do you like him?"

"Eliot is a nice kid, I guess. Well, he's a little crabby sometimes, but it could just be the first-day thing. I mean, it takes a kid a while to get used to a new person, right?"

"Right," Dad said.

"It's a little harder than I thought it would be, but that's okay. I'll survive, right?"

"Right," Dad said.

"We went to the pool and he almost ran away

66

but that's not a bad thing, is it? I mean, he was just being a normal two-year-old, right?"

"Absolutely, Maddie," Dad said. He reached over and rubbed Madison's shoulders. "You're going to be great at this. You're a star at whatever you try to do, honey. Trust me. I know these things. I'm your dad."

"Oh, Dad," Madison moaned again. "You're a big sap."

"Well, maybe I am," Dad said with a chuckle. "But I'm proud of it."

They joked around for a few moments more before Dad returned to the kitchen to finish making his meat loaf. Madison powered up her laptop and went online. Although her e-mailbox was empty, she surfed around for a while before dinner.

Madison logged on to bigfishbowl.com to see if the site had a chat room or a bulletin board just for baby-sitters. Now that she'd started her real job, she thought it would be smart to learn about good games to play and songs to sing with Eliot. But just as she typed the word BABY-SITTER into the site search engine, she got an Insta-Message.

```
<Wetwinz>: Hey girl what r u doing?
```

It was Fiona. Madison soon discovered that Aimee was also online. The three BFFs agreed to meet up in a private chat room they called SUNGRLS.

\<MadFinn\>: I'm so glad u r here

\<BalletGrl\>: How wuz baby-sitting???
Eliot???

\<MadFinn\>: He's a total QT . . .

\<MadFinn\>: when he's not throwing a
fit

\<BalletGrl\>: LOL

\<Wetwinz\>: Egg said he saw u @ the
pool w/him

\<MadFinn\>: yeah I looked 4 u 2
where were u?

\<BalletGrl\>: @ cyber caf w/my bros
ugh

\<Wetwinz\>: I had to help my parents
paint today and I read three more
books

\<MadFinn\>: :**(missed u

\<BalletGrl\>: Ben came into the
bookstore!

\<Wetwinz\>: no way!! U didn't tell
me that!

\<MadFinn\>: wow did u talk 2 him
this time

\<BalletGrl\>: he smiled at least
I wanted to ask him what
he wuz doing this summer
but

\<Wetwinz\>: u chickened out?

\<BalletGrl\>: sorta

\<MadFinn\>: that's ok maybe you'll
call him tomorrow

<Wetwinz>: HUP—Chet told me he
belongs 2 the pool
<BalletGrl>: Yeah well, I'll cross
my fingers
<MadFinn>: he would probably freak
if he knew u liked him since ur
like one of the prettiest girls
in seventh grade, Aim
<BalletGrl>: GET OUT!!!
<Wetwinz>: Maddie's right!
<BalletGrl>: yah yah whatever
hey what r u doing tomorrow
Maddie?
<MadFinn>: baby-sitting of course
<BalletGrl>: y do u have 2 do that
every single day
<Wetwinz>: bummer I thought we could
all hang out maybe go shopping or
something
<BalletGrl>: what about the wkend?
<MadFinn>: I can hang on Sun.
<Wetwinz>: ok but we can't hang
here Chet is having the guys over
<BalletGrl>: y don't u guys come
over here? We could hang out and
then go to Lake Dora together my
mom will drive
<MadFinn>: ok I'll check w/my dad
<Wetwinz>: me 2
<BalletGrl>: kool! Have fun @ work
tomorrow, Maddie!

```
<MadFinn>: thanx
<Wetwinz>: bye
<BalletGrl>: C u l8r
```

After her BFFs disappeared offline, Madison was pleasantly surprised to see an e-mail flashing in her mailbox.

```
From: Bigwheels
To: MadFinn
Subject: BABYSPITTING—HA HA
Date: Fri 20 June 6:02 PM
```

I've been thinking about ur babyspitting HA HA baby-sitting job. How's it going? When u said he was 2 and a half or something I knew u would probably have 2 deal with some kid who's screaming and whining about EVERYTHING. U have 2 hang in there even if it's hard. My mom told me once that being patient is the best thing u can do EVER. It WILL get better I swear. But don't ever ever let the kid bite you. That happened to my friend Josie once and she had 2 get a tetanus shot or something like that. Have u ever gotten a tetanus shot?

WBL or else :>) I'm going CRAZY

until camp!!! My little brother and sister are soooo annoying.

Yours till the baby sits,

Bigwheels, aka Vicki

Madison chuckled to herself. As usual, Bigwheels was getting dramatic. *Bite her?* Madison couldn't imagine Eliot doing that. But then again . . . so far he was full of surprises.

After hitting SAVE, Madison stretched backward on the bed and scanned the bookshelves. She felt like reading and regretted not getting a book or two out of the library with Fiona. The only books on the shelves here at Dad's were the books Madison didn't want to keep at home. She absentmindedly flipped through her old American Girl books and a copy of *Pippi Longstocking* that she'd read a hundred times in fourth grade.

"Rowrrrooooo!"

Phinnie, who'd been lying on the floor snoring the whole time, howled and jumped up onto the bed with Madison. Being so busy with her first day of Eliot meant that Phin hadn't gotten the attention he deserved. He wanted some now.

"Aw, Phinnie, are you a good boy?" Madison said in a squeaky voice. She rolled over and kissed his cold, wet nose by accident. "Blech!"

Phin panted back at her and jumped off the bed.

After chasing his tail for a little while, he trotted out of the room. Dinner was starting to smell yummy. Madison could smell it cooking and guessed he smelled it, too.

Madison wondered if she would be able to survive being a mother's helper. It had only been one day, and she was already stressed. And as good as the job was, would it take her away from everything and everyone she *really* wanted to enjoy over the summer? Was she up for this challenge?

Madison sat upright and faced the computer screen again.

It was time to type up a new file.

 Sink or Swim

Bigwheels is like my own personal baby-sitting adviser. She makes me feel way better about the whole Eliot sitch. I just need to keep up with him, that's all. That's what she said. But I can't believe it's only been a day with the Reeds—it feels like way more. How can I keep up? Will I sink or swim?

Rude Awakening: It should be called baby-running, not baby-sitting.

I thought being a mother's helper this summer would mean hanging by the pool and soaking up some rays! But this is a little more complicated than I expected.

And tomorrow is only day two.

Chapter 7

Madison rinsed off Eliot's spoon and handed it back to him. He was sitting up in his high chair, waiting for lunch, and Madison didn't want him to get cranky. She'd already spent the entire morning of her second baby-sitting day with Eliot, Tantrum Boy.

"NO!" Eliot cried. He sucked on the spoon and then hurled it across the kitchen. "NO! I want yogut!"

Carefully Madison spooned some pink cherry yogurt into a small plastic bowl. She handed it over to Eliot. He took one big scoop with the spoon and swallowed.

"Yummmmm!" he said, a huge smile spreading across his face.

Madison leaned back. *Success!* It had been impossible to get him to eat something for the last twenty minutes.

"Want some juice?" Madison asked, handing him a sippy cup filled with apple juice.

Eliot picked up the cup and sucked down some juice. Madison was relieved. Another success. And he was still smiling.

"You like that, huh?" Madison asked. She watched him take another long sip. Eliot squinted his eyes very tightly and leaned back in the high chair.

But before Madison could say or do anything else, Eliot threw the cup onto the floor with a loud grunt. Then he looked toward Madison. He wanted a reaction. She picked up the cup and tried to ignore him, replacing it on his tray.

But he only lifted it up once more. And threw it again—harder this time.

Madison gritted her teeth. "Don't throw," she told Eliot. "No throwing."

Eliot giggled. "Okay," he said. "Oh-kayeeee!"

Madison beamed. *Okay?* She couldn't believe he understood. She was making progress now. Eliot even took another quiet sip from the juice cup.

But the happy sipping didn't last.

After a few seconds he hurled the cup into the air. This time it crashed into the wall. The lid popped off. There was apple juice everywhere—splattered

74

on the wall, floor, and even onto Mrs. Reed's kitchen curtains. Madison felt nauseous. She wanted to scream.

HE-E-E-E-E-LP!

"Madison?" Mrs. Reed walked into the kitchen just in time to see Madison on hands and knees mopping up the spill. Eliot was leaning over the side of the high chair, dangling his spoon over Madison's head.

When she heard Mrs. Reed's voice, Madison didn't want to turn around. She dreaded the look. She dreaded the words, "You're the worst baby-sitter on the planet, and I don't want you to set foot in my house ever again!"

Of course, that wasn't what Mrs. Reed said.

In fact, she helped Madison clean up the mess and scolded Eliot for throwing things. She apologized to Madison for Eliot's angry outburst.

"He's been so cranky lately," Mrs. Reed said, wiping off his hands and face. "Ever since we had Becka . . ."

Eliot began to pound on his high-chair tray table as if it were his own personal drum set. Mrs. Reed unlatched his safety harness and lifted him out.

"What's wrong with you?" she said.

"Maybe he's mad at me," Madison said. "He doesn't really know me."

"Don't be silly," Mrs. Reed said, giving him a little kiss. "Okay, now that Becka is napping, Eliot,

Mommy is going to do some work around the house. You play nice with Madison, okay?"

Eliot wailed. "MAMA!" He leaned away as Mrs. Reed tried to point him in Madison's direction. "No, no, no!" he screamed.

Madison was afraid that with all Eliot's crying, Becka would wake up—and that somehow all of this chaos was her fault. She glanced up and saw that it was only eleven-thirty on the oven's digital clock. She still had half a day left to baby-sit.

Mrs. Reed handed Madison a sponge. "Wipe off the seat now. And do it anytime he uses the high chair, okay?"

Madison nodded. She looked forward to the days when all this new stuff was old stuff and she knew *exactly* what she was doing here.

After the kitchen incident, thankfully, things seemed to cool down for Eliot. He played with Legos in the living room for the next hour and even let Madison build a little Lego helicopter. They turned on a Wee Sing CD and started to sing along.

The more we sing together . . . together . . . the happier we'll be. . . .

Eliot bounced on his toes and shook his head.

"Aimee would love you," Madison told him. "You're a natural dancer."

"Dance-ah!" Eliot said.

They laughed together at the music.

The more we sing together . . . together. . . .

76

Madison reached over to grab his hand and dance with him, but Eliot's happy mood turned to instant distress.

"Nooooooooooooooooo!" he cried.

Madison leaned back. "What's wrong, Eliot?"

His face scrunched up like a wrinkled prune, and he let out a high-pitched screech. Naturally, Mrs. Reed came running.

"What is it? Eliot, what happened? Madison, what is it? Are you hurt?" she asked.

"Waaaaaaaaaaaaaaaaaaaaah!"

Madison turned and shrugged. "He just started crying for no reason."

"Oh, dear, there's always a reason," Mrs. Reed said.

Madison wasn't sure she believed that. After only one and a half days, Madison knew that Eliot liked to cry in the middle of lunch, in the middle of playing, in the middle of *everything*. There was no good reason for it except one.

Eliot didn't like Madison.

Even worse, Madison wasn't sure she liked him.

"Please stop screaming!" Mrs. Reed said, picking up Eliot and walking into the next room. "What's WRONG?" she asked him.

Eliot had drool and sniffle running out of each nostril. He sobbed into his mom's shoulder.

"I'm sorry," Madison kept saying. Her skin felt hot all over. "I can't seem to do anything right."

"No, no, no, I'm sorry," Mrs. Reed said. "We'll figure this out. I promise."

Mrs. Reed carried Eliot—still crying—upstairs for a nap. He crashed the moment he hit his mattress. Madison knew that because one moment he was blubbering and the next moment was total . . .

Silence.

Ahhhhh.

Becka was still asleep in her bassinet, too.

When she came back downstairs, Mrs. Reed didn't say anything at first. She pulled out a calendar daybook and opened it up on the kitchen table, pointing to the months of June and July.

"Starting next week, Eliot should be in better spirits," Mrs. Reed explained. "I think it's a good idea if we go over his schedule together. This week, Monday is musical jamboree, Tuesday and Wednesday are kiddie swim, Thursday is Pool Day, and Friday is games."

Pool Day? Madison was sure Egg had told her it would be during the weekend. What was it doing on a Thursday?

"Does Eliot go to Pool Day?" Madison asked, confused. This was one of the best events of the summer. She wanted to spend it with her friends. Not some baby.

"Eliot is competing in the kickboard swim for toddlers. It's one of a handful of events for the wee ones. I think they have more competitions for the older children. I'm sure you've done Pool Day other summers before, right?" Mrs. Reed asked. "You must have fond memories."

Madison felt a pang in the pit of her stomach. Memories?

"I think Eliot has a real shot at winning a kiddie ribbon," Mrs. Reed said.

"And what will I be doing?" Madison asked.

"What else? Spending time with Eliot, of course," Mrs. Reed said, smiling.

I'd rather be hanging out with Aimee and Fiona.
Watching Hart lifeguard.
Winning a Pool Day medal of my own!!!

Madison didn't say anything out loud. She just nodded and agreed with whatever Mrs. Reed said.

"I have to take Becka to the doctor," Mrs. Reed said. "You'll be fine." She smiled again. "Eliot will be in a good mood when he wakes up from his nap."

Forty minutes later, when Eliot awoke from his nap, he was in a much better mood. He even told Madison that her Lego helicopter was "goovy," which was his way of saying "groovy."

The remainder of the afternoon seemed to fly by after that. Soon it was time to head home and Madison was back at Dad's for dinner.

Despite all that had happened on day two, Madison didn't feel much like talking. Eliot whipped trucks at her head. What was that about? And he cried all the time. Madison didn't want Dad or Stephanie to think she was a total failure.

Most of all, Madison wanted to talk to Mom about it.

After a long, late dinner and dessert, Dad said Madison could telephone Mom in Australia. It was just about eight-thirty in Far Hills. That meant it was already twelve-thirty the next day where Mom was working! Madison hit a bunch of extra numbers to call long-distance. After a long wait, the phone on the other end finally began to ring.

"Mom?" Madison cried into the telephone. "Is that you?"

"Maddie?" Mom said. Her voice crackled with long-distance static. "What a surprise, honey bear!"

"I wanted to call because I missed your call yesterday and a lot has happened."

"I know I should have called last night . . .," Mom said.

"I got the mother's helper job," Madison said.

"You DID?" Mom squealed. "Hooray! I am so proud of you. I knew you could do it. How's it going? You just started?"

"Well, yeah . . ." Madison started to explain, but then the phone crackled and she wasn't sure if they were even still connected.

"Maddie?"

"Mom, are you still there?"

"Oh yes, honey bear—hold on a second—let me just—" Mom's voice was choppy. Madison glanced over at Dad. She wondered what he'd say if Madison told him that Mom had just put her on hold while she was calling halfway across the planet.

He'd die.

"Maddie, are you there?" Mom said. "I was just in the midst of a meeting when you called. A lunch meeting . . ."

"Oh, sorry," Madison said. "I know you're busy."

"No! I'm always here—wait, hold on another second, okay?" Mom interrupted Madison once again to speak to someone in her meeting.

Madison stared off into space.

Busy, busy, busy.

"Mommy?"

"Oh, Maddie, can I call you right back?" Mom asked.

"I miss you, Mom," Madison said, ignoring Mom's request. She wanted to talk and she wanted to talk *now*.

"Okay, honey bear. I'm sorry. Hold on for just a sec," Mom said.

Madison looked up from the phone to see Dad wink at her. Phinnie was zooming around the kitchen for scraps. Stephanie was drying the dishes.

She could hear Mom whispering to someone, rustling papers, and saying a loud "no." Mom was always doing fourteen things at once, Madison thought. Right now, Madison just wished one of those things was *her*.

"Honey bear!" Mom finally came back on the line. "I am so sorry. . . ."

Mom apologized for five minutes before they even started talking about real stuff again.

"So the reason I called you instead of waiting for you to call, Mom," Madison explained, "is because I'm so nervous about baby-sitting. It started out okay, but now it's been two days and he cries at everything. Yesterday at the pool he ran away. I don't think I'm very good."

"Oh, Maddie," Mom sighed. "Don't say that. Did you talk to Dad?"

"Uh-huh," Madison said. "You know, he told me all the good stuff like I was great and all that. But . . . I wanted to hear *your* voice. What do you think?"

"Oh, Maddie." Mom sighed again. "I wish I were there with you right now so I could lean over and give you the biggest hug in the world. Don't you know that you'll be an amazing mother's helper? You just need to give the baby-sitting some time. You've never really done this before. And little kids need time to warm up to you. I'm sure that Eliot will very quickly learn what fun the two of you will have together."

Mom's words were as good as a hug even though she felt so far away.

"When are you coming home?" Madison asked. Here she was talking about Eliot, but now *she* felt like the little kid.

Madison could hear Mom smile. Her voice went up. "Awww," Mom said sweetly. "I only just got here. I'm still in Sydney for a week. But it will go by fast. I promise."

After a long string of good-byes, Madison hung up the telephone. A little part of her felt empty—and even angry—inside. It was hard dealing with life without Mom by her side. It was tough not being in their house on Blueberry Street. It was hard not having Mom around to lend a hand or a hug when Madison felt super-insecure—like now.

While Stephanie and Dad talked about work and made a pot of tea, Madison sat curled up on the living room couch. She rubbed Phin's head and thought about her job. She imagined that Eliot was probably at home right now playing with his plastic trucks *alone*. Madison guessed that his mom wasn't available to him right now, either. She was off somewhere with Becka.

Madison wondered if maybe she and Eliot weren't so different after all.

And if that was true—then why couldn't they just get along?

The weekend flew by. Madison didn't get to spend as much time with her friends as she'd hoped. The planned trip to Lake Dora on Sunday was postponed again because of rain showers. Aimee, Fiona, and Madison hung out at Aimee's house and listened to CDs.

Madison tried to stop obsessing about the baby-sitting disasters of the previous week, but the whole time she was hanging out at Aimee's house on Blueberry Street, all she could think about was Eliot. He lived only a few houses away. Was he thinking up ways to drive Madison crazy when she came back on Monday?

Sunday afternoon, Madison had better luck distracting herself. The rain stopped, and she joined Stephanie and Dad for a long bike ride through Far Hills, stopping in briefly to see some new puppies at the animal clinic. Stephanie was acting buddy-buddy again, but Madison didn't mind so much anymore. It wasn't bad having Stephanie around, especially when Mom was missing in action.

Before dinner, Madison and Dad logged onto the computer together to play around. Dad demonstrated how to use the Flash Plug-in feature and showed Madison cool software to create homemade cards and paper. Madison copied some old down-loaded images of her favorite endangered animals to make flashy stationery.

But by the time Sunday night rolled around, Madison began gearing up for the week ahead with Eliot. And although she was exhausted from staring

at a computer screen for hours, she still made time
to write in her files.

 Eliot

I love Eliot.
Eliot loves me.
Eliot and I are going to be best, best
friends.
Stephanie has these self-help tapes that
talk about "cultivating patience like
crops" and "putting the joy back in enjoy."
I thought all that sounded so bizarre. Like
crops? What is that supposed to mean? I've
heard of meditation and yoga and all that,
but I now doubt whether this has any effect
on my life. And I know that Mom was super-
supportive to me last night, but I already
forgot half of what she said.
Rude Awakening: Thinking positive is
positively impossible.
I want to be upbeat about the whole
mother's helper thing. But I have this lump
in my throat like something is going to
happen.
And a lump is the worst kind of omen.

Chapter 8

By the time Monday morning rolled around, crying was no longer on Madison's mind. The day was bright and sunnier than sunny. She needed to make her mood sunny to go along with the day. Phin scooted all around Dad's apartment like he knew the weather was good—and Madison saw this as a positive omen. Finally. She was on the lookout for more good signs.

Dad drove her over to the Reed house. Madison arrived armed with her bathing suit, orange beach bag, and her own plush purple towel for today's trip to the Lake Dora pool. Mrs. Reed answered the door hurriedly but wore a happy, wide grin.

"Good morning," she chirped, inviting Madison inside. "You know, Madison, you don't have to ring the doorbell when you come. I'm expecting you. Just walk inside. That way if I'm in the middle of changing a diaper or picking up toys or just losing my mind . . ."

Her voice trailed off into laughter.

"Okay," Madison said, trying to take it all in.

"So how was the rest of your weekend?" Mrs. Reed asked. Her eyes darted around the room like she was looking for something—or someone.

Madison shrugged. "Nice except for the rain. I spent yesterday with my friends, my dog, and my dad. I like doing that. How was your Sunday?"

Mrs. Reed told Madison about the family's driving trip to visit Eliot's grandparents who lived two hours away. Thankfully, Mrs. Reed explained, he had been a good boy during the drive, napping and singing along with his Wee Sing CD. Becka was well behaved, too.

Eliot *good*? Madison could only hope that he'd make a repeat performance for her today. No sooner had thoughts of Tantrum Boy popped into her head than he appeared at the bottom of the stairs.

"Thwimming?" Eliot asked. Madison knew he must have recognized who she was from the week before, but he also seemed confused. In some ways starting this new week was like starting all over again. Eliot clung to his mom's leg, just like he had done the week before. He seemed on the verge of tears all over again.

Madison took a deep breath and remembered what Mom had said Saturday night.

It will take some time.

After lunch, Mrs. Reed packed the car up after Becka had a bottle, and everyone buckled into their seats. The drive over to Lake Dora took a little longer than usual due to morning traffic, but Eliot seemed content to hum to himself, suck on a shortbread cookie, and stare off into space. Becka fell asleep right away.

As usual, the pool was packed. Mrs. Reed and Madison negotiated the crowds and found empty chairs. More luck!

The good omens were piling up. Maybe I should have brought my rabbit's foot, too, Madison thought.

Positive thinking. Positively.

Hart, Egg, and Drew stood over by the lifeguard tower together. They hadn't see Madison yet. Madison noticed Aimee and Fiona, too, sitting nearby. There were a few empty chairs in their area. Madison wanted to ask Mrs. Reed if they could change seats so she could be closer to her friends.

But she didn't have a chance.

"Oh, it's getting late!" Mrs. Reed said as she smeared sunblock cream onto Eliot's arms and back. "I have to go to a 'baby and me' dance class inside the pool center for a while. You two will be okay here until I come back, right?"

Madison nodded. Eliot was playing with some blocks and a fake plastic cell phone he liked to carry around. Mrs. Reed motioned to Madison. "If you want, in a little bit you can go and get an *i-c-e c-r-e-a-m*." She smiled at Madison, swooped up Becka, and disappeared.

Eliot offered to show Madison one of his plastic sailboats that he kept in a little carrying case. Maybe today would be *g-o-o-d*.

Things even got better after a few moments when Hart walked by with Egg and Drew. Eliot remembered the boys from the week before and roared with giggles when Hart leaned over to tickle him again.

"So how's your boyfriend?" Egg teased again. He scruffed up the hair on top of Eliot's head.

Madison groaned. "Nice one, Egg."

But she didn't mind the wisecracks. Eliot was being a good boy. All his good behavior convinced Madison that maybe things were looking up. Maybe all of Mom's advice had sunk in? There were other mothers and mother's helpers around the pool, and she seemed to fit right in—sort of.

"Let's go see?" Eliot asked Madison.

"See what?" she asked.

"See! See!" Eliot said excitedly. He tugged on Madison's shorts.

Madison grabbed him right back. "See what, Eliot?" she asked again.

He made a face at her and tried to pull away. She kept her grip, but he kept pulling and groaning. They were standing up in front of everyone, and a few people started to stare.

"Eliot, shhh," Madison whispered. "Come back over here, okay?"

Now Eliot screamed, "No-o-o-o-o-o-o-o!" and yanked his arm away. Madison fell back onto a chair. He grabbed for her again. "No sitting. Come with me," he demanded, pulling her up off the chair.

Madison was trying to tug him gently back again when he broke free and swung out his arm. He hit her. Hard. When Madison stood back from him, her arm stung. Now several more people were staring. Madison could feel their eyes drilling holes through her back.

"I wanna see Mama," Eliot said.

Mama? At last she understood what all his fuss was about. He wanted his mother—not Madison. It was more proof that he hated her.

Positively.

"Mama just went away for a little while," Madison said softly, trying to reassure him. She gently took both of his wrists in her hands, but he pulled away again. Eliot lunged forward and grabbed Madison's bag from the chair. Almost everything fell out of her bag, and the bag itself went flying.

Splash.

Right into the pool.

Some kid in the deep end laughed out loud when he saw the bag float beside him. He hurled it up onto the pool deck, but it fell right back into the water. The lifeguard on duty blew a whistle.

Hart was first on the scene to retrieve the orange

bag. He leaned over the pool edge and saved
Madison's bag from sinking. She watched on in hor-
ror, knowing that her cheeks had turned blister red
between the sun . . . and the shame . . . of the passing moments. Her crush had saved the day.

"Funny," Eliot said, sounding an awful lot like a
parrot. "FUNNY! FUNNY! Funnnnnnnny!" He started
to laugh and went right back to his toy sailboat as if
nothing had ever happened.

Madison was relieved to have him calm down,
but at the same time her mind raced. What if Eliot
had thrown *himself* into the pool and not the bag?
she thought. What if Mrs. Reed had been there to
witness the whole sequence of events? Could she do
anything right when it came to baby-sitting?

Madison leaned over Eliot and patted him on the
back. "Are you okay now?" she asked quietly, pray-
ing for a quiet response.

Eliot just grinned. "Okay, Maddie," he said, as if
none of the commotion with the wet bag had ever
happened. "Wanna play tucks?"

Madison sat back in the chair, half in shock. But she
wasn't surprised by his sudden mood swing. She didn't
think it was strange that Eliot wanted to play. Madison
was stunned because Eliot Reed had said her name.

It was the very first time.

"So, you're hanging with babies now, huh?"
someone said from behind the chairs where Madison
and Eliot sat.

Madison turned to see her mortal enemy, Ivy Daly, and her drones, Rose "Thorn" and "Phony" Joanie. The trio stood with hands on their hips, gawking at Madison and Eliot. Ivy was dressed in a bikini with sparkles on it. It glittered in the sun. Ivy and both drones already had perfect tans.

"Hello, Ivy," Madison said, trying to be friendly even though she disliked Ivy and even though she was embarrassed. "Hi, Rose and Joanie," she said to the drones, too. "What are you guys doing here?"

Ivy smirked. "Having fun. What are YOU doing?"

Phony Joanie cackled. On closer inspection, Madison thought she looked bronze, as if she were wearing a tan out of a bottle.

Madison looked over at Eliot and sighed. "I'm having fun, too. I'm baby-sitting."

Unfortunately she didn't sound convincing, and she knew it.

"Sounds like fun," Ivy said, laughing some more. "Of course, I'd rather spend time with my friends my own age."

"Me too," Rose said.

"Me three," Joan said, giggling.

"Gee, where's Aimee or Fiona?" Rose asked.

"Are *they* baby-sitting, too?" Ivy couldn't stop laughing.

Madison was disappointed that she had no BFF to come to the rescue. Neither Aimee nor Fiona was anywhere to be seen—and here she was outnumbered three to one. The enemies giggled loudly, too, taking great pleasure in Madison's embarrassment. As the trio walked away in their perfect bathing suits and sunglasses that made them look sixteen instead of twelve, Madison guessed that Rose and Joan would follow Ivy for the rest of their lives and that right now Ivy was going off in search of Hart.

Meanwhile Madison was nowhere near Hart. She remained poolside with Eliot, her summer boyfriend.

Eliot held up a dirty Popsicle stick that he must have picked up off the ground. He put it into his mouth just in time for Madison to pull it out again.

"Stop! Stop!" she cried, taking the stick out of his hand.

"Why?" he asked. "Gimme. Gimme."

"It's dirty," Madison said. "Why don't we go get a real ice cream? Would you like that?"

Eliot's whole face lit up. "Yummy nice cream. I want chocklit."

Madison breathed deep.

It will take some time.

They walked over to the snack shop together.

One red, white, and blue pop and prepackaged fudge-ripple cone later, Madison and Eliot were both feeling better. Madison cruised back around toward their chairs and bumped back into her BFFs. She introduced them to Eliot.

Aimee was smitten. "Aren't you cute?" she kept

93

saying. Eliot didn't know what to make of all her cooing and aahing.

Fiona stuck out her hand. "Gimme five!" she said. Eliot promptly smacked her hand right back. She tried again and he smacked again.

"He is cute," Fiona said.

"Where have you been for the last hour?" Madison asked. "I saw you sitting over here, but then you vanished. I've been sitting over there by myself."

Eliot looked up at her with his big brown eyes as if to say, "Um, excuse me, but you're not by yourself."

"Well, I've been playing with Eliot," Madison corrected herself.

"Then let's hang out together right now," Aimee suggested. "I think I saw Ben Buckley in the recreation room. Let's go play Ping-Pong."

"We can find Egg, too," Fiona said. "I think lifeguarding is over for the day."

"But I can't bring Eliot into the recreation room," Madison said. "It's only for ages ten and up, I think."

"Bummer," Aimee said. She leaned in close to Fiona and Madison and pointed across the pool. "Look! I swear that was Ben. Oh, wow, we have to go find him. Come on."

Fiona grabbed Aimee's hand and giggled. "Let's go. Let's go!"

"Wait a second. Where are you going?" Madison asked. "I can't go."

She looked down at Eliot. He was tugging at his pants, and they were starting to fall down a little bit. Madison knew that meant he had a dirty diaper. Plus, there was ice cream all over his hands and face.

"Okay, we'll go but come back in a little while," Aimee said. "How's that?"

"Yeah, we'll come back," Fiona said.

Madison watched as Eliot stuck the entire ice cream cone into his mouth at once and started to chew. Madison needed to change his diaper and wipe off his stickiness.

"Okay. But if I miss you, can we meet later?" Madison asked. "Will you guys be online this afternoon or tonight?"

"Maybe," Aimee said. "We have a family dinner tonight for my visiting aunt and uncle."

"I'm around," Fiona said. "Call me from your dad's later. Maybe I can even come over."

"Oh, good." Madison nodded, walking away. "See you later, then!"

"Bye," her BFFs said in unison before scurrying over to the recreation room.

Madison looked down and saw that Eliot had eaten his entire ice cream by now. He was wearing half of it. His diaper was officially falling off, too.

"Was that yummy or what?" Madison asked as she dragged Eliot toward the bathrooms. "You have chocolate on your face, do you know that?" She tried to lean down and wipe off Eliot's chin and the corners of his mouth, but he protested—loudly. Then she took him inside to change the diaper.

When they came back out again, the two ran into Mrs. Reed and Becka. Madison was relieved. The four spent the remaining time lying around in the sun quietly together. Eliot even played peekaboo with his little sister.

When the day was done, Mrs. Reed gave Madison a ride back home to Dad's apartment. Everything was going great in the car until Eliot pinged another one of his miniature toy trucks at her head.

"Ouch!" Madison yelled.

As if on cue, Eliot started to cry for no reason.

"I think he's teething again," Mrs. Reed said. "Eliot, are you teething again?"

Madison shrank down into the seat. What did I do to deserve this? she thought. Since she'd started her summer job, she hadn't caught a break. Eliot was one test after another.

"See you tomorrow!" Mrs. Reed said as she let Madison off. Eliot was *still* crying a little bit in the backseat.

"See you tomorrow," Madison said as the car pulled away. Inside she was thinking: Oh, goody.

Phin greeted Madison at the door with hysterical panting and tail wagging. Madison picked him up and kissed his ears because she was so happy about the warm reception. They went for a short walk down the street and into a small park called

Shady Glen around the corner from Dad's place. There was a fenced-in dog run in the park. Phin trotted through the fence gate and began to sniff wildly at the ground. This was dog heaven. He alternated hanging out with a dachshund named Frankie and an Irish setter named Scruff. Someone let him join in a game of Frisbee, too, even though he didn't catch the disk. He just raced back and forth in the dirt with a bunch of other dogs.

It was nice to look after someone who wasn't crying or fussing or throwing a fit, Madison thought as she watched the dogs playing. Dogs were definitely easier than little boys.

When they returned from the walk, Dad greeted the pair at the door with a big hello and a big bowl of freshly popped popcorn.

"Snack time!" Dad announced. "Hey, Maddie, I rented a movie for tonight—a scary one. Alfred Hitchcock's *The Birds*. You haven't seen it yet, have you?"

Madison shook her head and grinned. Dad always acted so goofy when he rented old movies for them to watch together. He liked telling bad jokes and watching thrillers. But watching scary movies with Dad was the best because Madison could scream and squeeze his hand and feel safe no matter what.

"Can Fiona come over and watch, too?" Madison asked.

"Sure!" Dad said. "Why don't you call her? I can go pick her up."

"Okay. But is it all right if I go online for a little bit before dinner first?" Madison asked.

"Okeydoke." Dad nodded. "Let's eat in an hour. Sound good?"

After grabbing a handful of the popcorn, Madison went straight for her laptop while Phin went straight for his water dish and chew toys.

Madison logged on to bigfishbowl.com and opened her e-mailbox. She had an urgent e-mail to send.

From: MadFinn
To: Bigwheels
Subject: Put a Fork in Me
Date: Mon 23 June 5:15 PM

Put a fork in me. I'm done! My list of baby-sitting disasters is growing longer. Not only did Eliot throw my favorite woven orange straw bag into the pool today, but he also SPIT UP on me a little bit after we had ice cream. I told Mrs. Reed, but she didn't seem to think it was a big deal. Just tell that to the puke spot on my T-shirt! Will I ever get the hang of this? I think the worst part of all is changing diapers.

Lucky for me he is good about being still when I change him because it takes me twice as long as it takes his mom to get the diaper off and a new one on.

I just realized that I'm writing this to u on ur first day at horse camp so I hope u can write back soon. My dad and his girlfriend and my mom are all trying to cheer me up. My friends don't really seem to get it, though. They're too busy chasing boys at the pool, and I think that is so lame (even though I secretly wish I were chasing boys, too—and not ones who are 2!).

When u baby-sat b4, what was the worst thing that ever happened to you? Just when I think I've experienced the worst, something else crazy happens.
Write back & tell me about the horses. Have u gone riding yet?

Yours till the pony expresses,

Maddie

Chapter 9

"Looks like the pool will be closed again," Dad said, sipping his cup of coffee. "They say the rain is supposed to keep up most of the day."

As Madison gazed out the window, her entire body ached with dread. It was hard enough keeping track of Eliot at the pool, but at least he had other kids to see and places to go there. What was she supposed to do with him if they were stuck inside all day?

Dad leaned over and kissed the top of her head. "Hey, Maddie," he joked. "Why can't you go over to the Shady Glen dog run today?"

Madison made an annoyed face. "I don't know, Dad. Why?"

"Because you might step in a poodle!" Dad chuckled. His own bad jokes always cracked him up.

But something about Dad's joke made Madison reconsider her way of thinking. What was she doing sitting around worrying? The rain was her big chance. She wasn't going to let Eliot ruin another day for her . . . or him. She could get creative! This was the kind of baby-sitting challenge Mom was talking about. Maybe Madison needed to give Eliot some more things to do.

The digital clock in the living room read 7:13. Madison had an hour to get ready and figure out her plan of attack.

After pulling on her plaid shorts and pink T-shirt, Madison logged on to Dad's flat-screen computer in the living room. He had a super-speed connection, so the Internet was easier to access than the dial-up connection she sometimes used with her laptop. She quickly typed in her search words.

Rainy Day Activity 2 Years Old Fun

The screen popped up 1,812 hits. Madison selected the first few for ideas. She scribbled notes down on a scratch pad sitting on Dad's desk.

Bath toys in the sink, towel on floor, take off shirt

Color in paper plates—need nontoxic markers and plates

Go fishing with magnets in middle of floor?

Cookie cutter sandwiches—stars and moons

I could always go outside and play with Eliot in the poodles, too, Madison thought. She chuckled at Dad's joke again. It was time to go.

Mrs. Reed seemed flustered when Madison walked right into the house, even though she'd told Madison it was fine to do that.

"You startled me," Mrs. Reed said.

Becka was sitting in her lap, drinking from her morning bottle. Eliot was playing with the cushions on the sofa.

"My husband had to leave earlier than usual today," she said. "So I'm a little out of sorts. He usually feeds Becka the morning bottle. Now I'm running late. . . ."

"What can I do to help?" Madison asked.

"Can you take Eliot out of here? He keeps jumping on my shoulders, and I just can't get anything done with her. Plus, I think they're both a little out of whack with all this rain. Unfortunately, we won't be going to the pool today. You can go outside with him if you want. . . ."

"No problem. I'll figure it out," Madison said. She

moved toward Eliot. "Good morning, Eliot! Hey, it's Maddie. Do you remember me?"

Eliot smiled. "Course I 'member you! See my slide?" He pointed to the sofa cushions.

"Why don't we go and play with your trucks in the other room?" Madison suggested.

Eliot looked up at her and smiled again. "Okay, Maddie, we can play tucks," he said. Madison was encouraged by his willingness to play along with her. He even said, "Bye, Mama," without throwing a hissy fit.

"Bye, sweetheart," Mrs. Reed said. She looked super-relieved and cuddled Becka closer to her middle. "I'll see you two in a little while."

The truck room, formerly known as the Reed dining room, was a total mess. Madison knelt down and started to pick up the teeny cars and trucks one by one.

"Hey! No!" Eliot cried. "Those are tuck stops. Don't move."

"These are what?" Madison asked. "Truck stops? How did you figure these out?"

"No touching!" Eliot cried.

Madison dumped all the cars that were in her hand onto the floor again. "Sorry," she said. Instead of getting frustrated, she tried harder to understand what Eliot wanted next. "Should we put them back together?"

They replaced all the truck stops and played

103

unloading and loading games for about half an hour. Then Eliot jumped up and announced to the room that he was ready to go "thwimming."

Madison gulped. "I'm sorry, Eliot," she said. "But it's rainy, so we have to stay here and play."

"No thwimming?" he asked.

Madison shook her head. "No. But we can find other things to do together, can't we?"

"Like what?" Eliot asked. "I want thwimming. I want Mama."

"Well, Mama's busy right now, so why don't we make up some other games together?"

"Like what? What?" Eliot asked again. "WHAT?" he wailed.

"Is everything okay?" Mrs. Reed called out from the other room. "Madison?" She was acting as anxious as her kids. Madison had to keep her cool and stay focused.

MAKE ELIOT HAPPY.

"We're okay," Madison called to Mrs. Reed. Then she turned to Eliot. "I have an idea. Since we can't go swimming, let's do something else and get wet," Madison said.

"Go outside?" Eliot said with a big grin.

Madison glanced out the window at the rain. It was a total downpour. They could survive playing in the yard during a sprinkle, but this was too, too wet.

"How about we play in the bathroom?" Madison asked.

Eliot was intrigued, so he nodded and followed Madison upstairs.

Eliot had his own bathroom with his own little stepping stool up to the sink. Madison was happy about that, because the Web article she'd read about this particular activity called for a teeny stool just like his. Overhead, in the bathroom ceiling, was a skylight window. The rain plinked overhead. It was almost like being in the middle of the downpour—without getting wet.

But Eliot was about to get *very* wet.

Madison threw a thick towel down on the floor and pushed Eliot's stool up to the sink. He was busy gathering his tub toys. Madison told him to get his plastic boats, too. His eyes were glimmering with excitement.

"What are you two up to?" Mrs. Reed asked from the bathroom doorway.

Becka looked around the room, wide-eyed.

Madison explained, and Mrs. Reed smiled. "You're terrific! What a great idea!" she told Madison. "You already know how much he likes playing with his boats, huh? What do you think, Eliot?"

"Mama gonna play in the sink!" he cried.

Mrs. Reed laughed. She told Madison that Eliot could take off his T-shirt and strip down to a diaper so he wouldn't get his clothes soaked. Of course, Eliot *loved* that. He pulled his shirt right off and started to hop around the bathroom like a kangaroo.

Madison filled the sink with water and soap bubbles. Eliot battled his boats. Water went everywhere, but Madison didn't mind one bit. Eliot was giggling with each dunk.

They had so much fun together in the bathroom that an hour flew by. Soon it was time for lunch. Eliot whined a little about stopping, but Madison convinced him that it wouldn't be so bad. She was planning another creative idea for lunch—the next item on her list—making little sandwiches and cutting them into shapes with cookie cutters.

The rain outside seemed to be letting up a little. Mrs. Reed put Becka down for a nap. Madison could tell that Eliot was the happiest he'd ever been when Madison was with him, but he still cried out a little at times for his mother. Unfortunately, whenever she tried to spend a few moments with Eliot, Madison noticed that Mrs. Reed always got distracted. Eliot asked her to read him a book, and she passed the task along to Madison. He asked Mrs. Reed to play Legos, but she had to get the phone. He asked for a hug, and she had to run and check on the baby.

By late afternoon, Mrs. Reed's casual brush-offs seemed to be making Eliot crankier than cranky. He lost interest in reading books and playing toys with Madison. She suggested they play with the boats in the sink again, and he stuck out his tongue. She asked him what *he* wanted to do, and he pulled Madison's hair.

Of course, Madison knew what he really wanted. But that was the one thing she couldn't do for him. Eliot didn't want to color, and Madison had no luck fishing with magnets, another game the Internet suggested. She only had two refrigerator magnets, and they didn't work very well at all.

When Mr. Reed arrived home, Madison called Dad to say that she'd be going over to Aimee's house and that he should pick her up there.

And even though Eliot was moody when Madison left, he seemed a little sad to say good-bye. It was the first time Madison thought he even noticed that she was leaving.

"Buh-bye, Maddie," Eliot said, waving to Madison as she sprinted out into the rain. "See you tomollow."

Madison chuckled. "See you then. Bye, Mrs. Reed!"

She leaped over a few giant puddles and walked down the street toward Aimee's house. Blossom was spread out on her belly on the Gillespie porch, sniffing at the rainy air.

"Blossom!" Madison cried. She leaned down to kiss her big ears, and Blossom shook her head.

"Maddie!" Aimee said as she pulled open the door. "I was so glad you called. Come inside!"

Two of Aimee's brothers were inside watching TV and eating homemade vegetarian nachos. Every meal in the Gillespie house was a tribute to health food. Even TV snacks here were healthy.

"Wanna go out on my roof?" Aimee asked Madison.

"It's kind of wet outside, Aim," Madison said. "Can we just hang here and make milk shakes or smoothies or something?"

Aimee nodded. "I have something to tell you," she said in a singsong voice. Her eyes bugged out wide.

"What?" Madison said, taking off her coat. "What is it?"

"He called me," Aimee said.

"Who?" Madison asked.

"Who do you think? BEN!" Aimee said. "He called me this afternoon. He said that he's been thinking about calling me since the summer started."

"Get OUT!" Madison cried.

They both screamed with delight.

"So what are you going to do now?" Madison asked. "Are you guys going on a date or something?"

"A date?" Aimee said. "No way. He just wanted to see if I would be at the pool tomorrow. If it's not raining, of course. And he DID see me that day when I was sitting there in the hat. Isn't that cool?"

Madison sat down on Aimee's bed and sighed. "You are so lucky, Aim," she said. "You like someone, and he likes you back."

"We only talked once. He got my number from Egg, can you believe it?"

"I can't believe Egg would give out your number when he makes fun of us so much," Madison said.

"I think maybe Fiona told him to do it," Aimee said. "But whatever. He called. Ben called!"

As usual, Aimee danced around her room.

Madison joined right in.

"I haven't seen you in this good a mood in weeks," Dad said to Madison over dinner. He had picked up some food at McDonald's on his way home from a meeting.

Madison bit into a french fry and stared off into space.

"I haven't been in a good mood, Dad," she said. "But I think I've turned a corner. I think."

"Good for you," Dad said, tossing one of his fries onto the carpet. Phin was begging at the table again.

"Dad! I'm trying to get him to stop begging, and you're not helping when you feed him scraps!" Madison complained.

Dad laughed. "You should put Phin on a seafood diet," he said.

Madison groaned. "Yeah, Dad, so every time he sees food, he'll eat. Ha-ha-ha. You're so funny, I forgot to laugh."

"You can't fault me for trying," Dad said with a wink.

After they did the dishes, Madison went online to see if anyone had written her e-mail. She was pleasantly surprised.

FROM	SUBJECT
✉ Wetwinz	BBQ at Our Place
✉ GoGramma	Howdy
✉ ff_BUDGEFILM	I Miss You
✉ Bigwheels	Here's What I Think

Fiona, aka Wetwinz, had sent e-mail to Madison, Aimee, and everyone else in their group of friends. She and Chet were organizing a barbecue at their house on Saturday. They would be having grilled food and games in their backyard. The Waters family was still in the middle of repainting the old Victorian house they lived in, but that didn't matter. The party was on! Madison was happy to know that was one summer event she wouldn't have to miss. She made a note in her calendar and planner.

Gramma Helen also had written to check in and say hello. Madison wrote a quick note back about the summer job, Eliot the Tantrum Boy, and hanging out with Dad while Mom was away on business. As she hit SEND, Madison realized that she needed to write more often to Gramma. She made another note in her calendar and planner.

The third message was from Mom. Madison read

and printed it out so she could carry it in her pocket or stick it in her bag. It would be like having Mom right there along with her.

```
From: ff_BUDGEFILM
To: MadFinn
Subject: I Miss You
Date: Tues 24 June 2:51 PM
Honey bear, I have been thinking
about you all day. It's very late
here right now, and I keep wishing
I could be there to talk and try to
help you feel better. Trust me when
I say that the summer will be here
and gone before you know it. And
your experience with Eliot will be
very rewarding. Australia is a
wonder! I have to take you here
sometime. Of course, as you know,
it's winter here while it's summer
there. It's so strange being on the
other side of the world from you.
But I'll be home soon! Give Phin a
hug for me.


All my love, Mom
```

As great as Mom's e-mail was, the very best message was the last one.

From: Bigwheels
To: MadFinn
Subject: Here's What I Think
Date: Tues 24 June 5:09 PM

Maddie you would not believe how beautiful my camp is. We have these great cabins that are easy to get to and we have horseback lessons twice a day and crafts and a whole bunch of other activities. They even have computer labs where u can talk online with friends from home.

You asked me have I ever had any bad experiences baby-sitting my cousin? Duh! Of course! One time I was watching her and she stuck a ham sandwich and a carrot into the VCR. The machine ate it and I was picking out these little orange pieces. It was awful. Another time we were painting and she threw a jar of paint at the wall and it broke. There was green everywhere even on these expensive chairs. Her mom yelled at me forever for that one. You can STILL see some of the green on their rug. I think that your stories this summer probably top mine. IIWM I'd keep files on them all!!

I am so glad that I can write b/c
it makes a big difference knowing
ur out there. I would go crazy if I
couldn't write to you for a whole
month.

Thanks for being such a cool
keypal.

Yours till the horse shoes,

Victoria, aka Bigwheels

Madison hit SAVE. Not even the rain could
dampen her spirits today.

Between Mom and Bigwheels, Madison was
finally starting to believe that this summer baby-
sitting job would work out.

She was finally starting to believe in herself.

Chapter 10

Madison couldn't believe that Stephanie was meeting Dad for breakfast *again*. Dad said Stephanie was coming over to help with an important business presentation. Of course, he couldn't get anything done in the middle of his morning rush. He ran around the kitchen wearing his good pants and undershirt but no socks and no dress shirt, because he hadn't ironed it yet.

Madison chuckled to herself as she slurped down her bowl of Toasty-Os. This was the Dad she remembered from mornings at home back before the big D. This was the Dad who used to be married to Mom. Crazy Dad.

She missed seeing him every day.

"Should I wear the blue or red tie, Maddie?" Dad asked.

Madison shrugged. "What about the orange one?" she said.

"Orange? What?" Dad looked panicked for a moment. Then he stopped in his tracks. "Oh, I see. What a joker."

He came over and gave her a huge squeeze.

Ding-a-ling. Ding-a-ling.

"Dad, you have to do something about that doorbell. It sounds so lame," Madison said.

Phin leaped up, barking at the doorbell like an attack dog. Once he saw Stephanie, however, the pug turned to mush. He loved Stephanie because she always gave him fake bacon strips and scratched his back in exactly the right place.

"Good morning, troops!" Stephanie said, swinging her briefcase onto the counter.

"Hey," Dad said, giving her a little kiss. Madison cringed. It was way too weird to watch her parents kiss, let alone watch them kiss other people.

"Aren't you dressed yet? Where's your shirt?" Stephanie asked.

"Oh no! I knew there was something I forgot!" Dad cried. He dashed out of the room like the scarecrow in *The Wizard of Oz*, all floppy and confused.

Madison took another bite of cereal and smiled at Stephanie. "He's been standing around like that for a half hour," Madison said. "What a dork."

Stephanie giggled. "That's what I love about him," she said. "So how's the baby-sitting going?"

"Okay," Madison said. "Yesterday was better, but Eliot isn't very happy a lot of the time. I'm learning to deal with that."

"Isn't happy? Why not?" Stephanie asked.

"He cries a lot. He doesn't like it when I change his diaper. He hates it when we try to sing songs, like he knows I'm a really bad singer. Is that possible? And he threw my bag into the pool the other day," Madison said.

"He's two and a half, right?" Stephanie asked.

"Yeah," Madison said. "What does that have to do with it? He hates me. I know when someone hates me, and HE hates me."

Stephanie poured herself a cup of coffee from the drip machine on the counter. "Maddie," she said. "No two-year-old hates anyone. He just doesn't know you. I'm sure that he's upset about something, but I bet it isn't you."

"How do you know that?" Madison asked.

"You said he has a new sister, right? He probably is jealous of her."

Madison's jaw dropped. A giant neon bulb went on inside her head. Of course *that* was it! Eliot didn't hate Madison. He hated Becka.

But that didn't make sense, either.

Eliot loved his little sister. He hugged her whenever he had the chance. He gave her one of his favorite stuffed animals. He even liked watching Becka fall asleep.

Madison put her head in her hands. "Stephanie, it must be me. I try everything I know to make him happy. And it's only been a week or so, but I think that maybe this isn't the right job—"

"Don't say that!" Stephanie said, interrupting. "This is all a minor setback."

Madison knew this was one of those bonding moments when Stephanie got this "trust me, I know what you're talking about" look in her eye.

"What do you know about baby-sitting?" Madison asked.

"What do I know about baby-sitting? You name it. I baby-sat in high school and college to help pay bills," Stephanie explained. "And don't forget I have a family of a hundred or so relatives—cousins, nieces, nephews—most of whom I baby-sat at some point in my life."

Madison had forgotten how big Stephanie's family back in Texas was. She couldn't imagine having that many people turn up at a barbecue or other family event.

"I baby-sat this little girl once and she would not smile. Not once. Not ever."

"Come on," Madison said. "Every baby smiles."

Stephanie shook her head. "Oh no, not Jessie. That was her name. And of course, just like you, I thought she HATED me."

Madison listened close. "So what did you do?" she asked.

"I became her friend," Stephanie explained. "When Jessie was grumpy, I just let her be. And when I didn't *force it*, she came around. One day Jessie just grinned right at me. Needless to say, I melted."

"But if Eliot is only two . . . how can I be his friend? He doesn't want me. He wants his mom," Madison said.

"Maddie, little Eliot needs you to be his friend more than anything, no matter what he does. He doesn't know about being bad or hate yet. Like you said, he's only two! And sure he wants his mom, but he'll get used to you. He'll realize that you're the one giving him special attention. Be patient."

Everything Stephanie was saying was like what Mom had said. Although Madison didn't like to admit it, Stephanie really *was* a little like a fill-in mom while the real one was in Australia. She took time to really listen.

"Madison Finn!" Dad shouted from the doorway. His shirt was ironed, buttoned, and cuff-linked, and he was wearing the red tie. "We have to go, young lady. You're due at Mrs. Reed's in ten minutes."

Madison leaped up from where she'd been sitting and lunged for Stephanie. She held on tight.

"Thanks, Steph," Madison said. "I know sometimes I'm not so patient with you, either, and—"

"Madison, go to work and forget about me. Focus on Eliot." Stephanie patted Madison on the shoulder. "I'll see you later."

"What's going on?" Dad asked.

"Girl talk," Stephanie said with a wink.

"What's this? I go to iron one shirt and suddenly you two are having some secret conversation?"

Madison kissed Dad on the cheek. "We were talking about YOU, Dad," she teased, racing out of the room to fix her hair and stuff a bathing suit and towel into her bag. They'd be hanging out at the Lake Dora pool today. The sun was shining hot, and the temperature outside was at least seventy-five degrees at eight-thirty in the morning.

Believing in the karma of the universe was how Madison explained Eliot's mood that day. He was happier than she'd ever seen him, and Madison became convinced that was all because of her talk with Stephanie that morning.

Madison had prepared herself for another battle of wills, expecting Eliot to be running around the pool like he'd done before. But today he was content to stay close to the chairs where Madison sat with Mrs. Reed and Becka.

Sometime around noon, Madison took him for a long walk. He was quiet and curious. It made it easier to have a real conversation.

"Are you excited about Pool Day?" Madison asked.

"Yah, yah." Eliot nodded. "I can thwim! Mama says."

Madison nodded right back. "And you're a good swimmer with your horsey on, right, Eliot?"

"Right, Maddie," he said with a smile.

They walked down by Lake Dora and watched some kids testing out a couple of new remote-control sailboats. Eliot liked standing down by the lake water and squishing sand through his fingers and toes. Madison let him wade into the wake of the water a little bit until he got nervous. Then they decided—together—to head back to the pool.

Mrs. Reed was sitting around the pool with a good friend who also had an infant. They were stretched out in the shade under a striped umbrella with the babies fast asleep on their bellies. Madison waved from way across the pool and waited for a wave back.

That's when it happened.

Eliot, who had been walking slowly next to Madison, ran ahead toward the pool. Madison let out a little gasp. He wasn't wearing his inflatable horsey and she could see him not looking and running too fast toward the edge. . . .

"Eliot!" Madison called out.

Thwoomp!

Before he could reach the edge, Eliot tripped on the pool deck.

Splat!

Madison saw Mrs. Reed stand up across the way, one hand holding Becka and the other hand covering her mouth like she was gasping. She'd heard Madison's cry.

By now a few other kids ran over toward Eliot.

"Hey!" someone shouted. A whistle blew. "No running!"

It was Hart yelling. The lifeguard director sent him over.

Madison raced over to Eliot, who pushed himself up onto his knees.

"AAAAAAAAH!" he wailed.

He had a small scrape on his shin and a teeny little bump on his knee. There was no real bleeding. He would probably get a bruise.

Mrs. Reed came running.

Hart leaned down to made sure that nothing else had happened to Eliot. He was crying loudly by now.

"Eliot, are you okay?" Madison asked.

She expected him to look at her with that usual crabby stare, the kind he'd been giving her since their relationship began. Or at least for Eliot to scream, "I want my mama."

But he didn't—at least not at that moment.

As Hart helped Eliot to get up, Eliot turned right toward *Madison* and extended his arms.

"Maddie!" he cried. Was he looking for a hug? Madison grabbed and held close.

Mrs. Reed arrived on the scene moments later. "Is

121

everything okay?" she asked. "Oh, poor Eliot. Mama told you not to run at the pool."

Eliot sniffled. "Maddie! Maddie!" he said, burying his face in Madison's neck.

Mrs. Reed leaned in. "Well, at least he's okay," she said, taking Eliot into her own arms. He was still crying, but "Maddie" had changed to "Mama."

"I'm so sorry, Mrs. Reed," Madison said.

"Accidents happen," Mrs. Reed replied. "Just as long as he's okay. We're all okay. Right?"

When the crowd had left and the pool medic checked out Eliot's scrapes, Madison and Mrs. Reed took him back over to the chairs. Mrs. Reed's friend was still watching Becka.

"Boo-boo," Eliot said, trying to pick at his Band-Aid.

"Don't touch," Mrs. Reed said, swatting at his little hand. "I know it hurts, sweetie. But that will make it all better."

Eliot looked up at Madison. "Boo-boo," he said.

Madison went to rub his back, but he pulled away.

"Mama!" Eliot wailed.

Mrs. Reed turned to him. "What, honey? Why don't you play with Madison?"

"No, I don't wanna!" Eliot said.

Madison sat back in her chair and took a deep breath. She could feel the perspiration rolling down her back. It was more than the heat. It was nerves.

"I'm sorry," she said to Mrs. Reed again. "It's all my fault."

"Oh, Madison," Mrs. Reed said. "He'll get over it. Don't worry. Like I said, it was an accident. You'll be more careful next time. Tomorrow is another day."

Madison wasn't sure she'd even make it to tomorrow.

She'd been baby-sitting for less than a week, and she already had page after page of disaster files.

What could possibly happen next?

Madison didn't tell Dad about the pool incident right away when she got home. She wanted to chat with someone else about it first.

Amazingly, Bigwheels was online and she could chat, too, from camp.

That was a good omen.

Madison wrote quickly, explaining what had happened at Lake Dora that afternoon. Bigwheels was very understanding.

```
<MadFinn>: so she told me not 2
   worry but I am
<Bigwheels>: he didn't get hurt tho
<MadFinn>: FYA—Hart saw the whole
   thing & prob thinks I'm the
   world's worst sitter EVER
<Bigwheels>: NT
<MadFinn>: thanx for talking I know
   ur @ camp
```

<Bigwheels>: I'm not the only 1
   who's online w/keypals
<MadFinn>: I feel so %-Z
<Bigwheels>: b/c you are!
<MadFinn>: VVF
<Bigwheels>: soooo what else is gnu
<MadFinn>: my mom is still in
   Austrailia wait how do u spell
   that?
<Bigwheels>: Australia
<MadFinn>: well my dad and his gf
   are here, which is kool beans
   even when they KISS in front of
   me
<Bigwheels>: ONNA
<MadFinn>: how many times have u
   kissed someone?
<Bigwheels>: 1 and it wasn't very
   long
<MadFinn>: me 2
<Bigwheels>: so what will u do
   tomorrow @ baby-sitting???
<MadFinn>: put on a Barney costume
   LOL oh y is it soooo hard?!!
<Bigwheels>: I think ur great &
   Eliot will think so soon
<MadFinn>: thanks :-)
<Bigwheels>: just don't let him put
   carrots in the DVD player LOL
<MadFinn>: have fun horseback riding
   2day

```
<Bigwheels>: tx see ya
<MadFinn>: TTFN
```

Madison said her good-byes and was about to log off completely when her computer pinged. Someone else sent her an Insta-Message.

```
<BalletGrl>: Maddie! We're meeting @
   Freeze Palace 4 ice cream in an
   hour wanna come?
```

Madison couldn't believe it. She hit REPLY and sent an Insta-Message right back.

```
<MadFinn>: I will TOTALLY be there!
   C U! :-)
```

She disconnected and dashed to her closet. She would have to change out of her clothes. She yanked a sleeveless ruffled blouse and a patchwork skirt off a hanger. She hardly ever wore skirts anymore.

But Madison wanted to look extra pretty, just in case a certain someone else was at Freeze Palace, too.

125

Dad suggested that he take Phin for walk *and* drop off Madison at Freeze Palace along the way.

"We can stop at Vito's Italian Ristorante for a slice of pizza, too," he said. "A girl has to eat some dinner before her ice cream, right?"

The night was perfect, with a tiny, warm breeze. Madison could smell garlic in the air outside the pizzeria. She waited with Phin at an outdoor table while Dad got the food.

Across the street, Madison spied her least-favorite person on the planet walking along with her parents. But Poison Ivy wasn't dressed in short shorts and a halter top now. She had on a modest sundress instead. Her mom probably picked it out for

126

her, Madison thought. She wondered if Ivy was headed toward Freeze Palace, too. She hoped not.

"Two slices coming right up!" Dad announced. He ran back inside to get two cans of root beer, too.

"Thanks for dinner, Dad," Madison said.

"Did I mention that you look ravishing this evening?" Dad said. "I'm the luckiest guy in all of Far Hills. . . ."

"Daddy!" Madison said, giving him a tap across the table. "Quit it. You're embarrassing me."

Dad smirked. "I'm just so proud of you," he said.

The pizza was delicious, and Madison loved her outside picnic pizza meal with Dad. When she took her last bite, she smiled at him.

Dad smiled back and checked his watch. "Let's go. Your friends are waiting."

The line outside Freeze Palace was down the block, as usual. But they had set up extra tables and picnic benches in the back courtyard. Dad and Phin left Madison at the door. He said he would pick her up again at eight.

A crowd of her friends was gathered at one of the picnic tables way in the back. Everyone was squished together on the benches. Egg and Fiona were sitting together on two chairs off to the side of the table, and Hart was standing.

"Hey, Maddie!" Fiona said. "We were wondering if you'd come."

"How's your boyfriend?" Egg teased.

Madison growled. "Very funny, Egg."

"Hey, Finnster," Hart said. His teeth flashed perfect white as he smiled.

Madison smiled back, shaking off the goose bumps she felt as he looked at her with his brown eyes. His skin was nut colored from the sun.

"You!" Aimee jumped up and gave Madison a fake punch. "I miss you, Maddie! We never see you anymore."

"That's not true," Madison said. "Is it?"

"I had something to tell you . . ." Aimee started to say. But then she got distracted. "Oh! He's here."

Madison turned to see Ben Buckley walking into Freeze Palace. The other guys at the table grunted their hellos. Ben put up a hand as if to say, "Hey."

"Hi, Madison," Ben said.

Aimee was having a hard time keeping her feet on the ground.

"I'm so glad you came. Wait, come over here, I saved you a seat." Aimee grabbed Ben's elbow, and they went over to the other side of the picnic table.

Madison couldn't believe that Aimee would have saved him a seat and not saved *her* a seat. Meanwhile Hart and Drew were arm wrestling at the table. Madison stood there alone.

"Don't just stand there. Pull up a chair," Chet said. He and Dan Ginsburg were stuffing their faces with ice-cream sundaes.

Unfortunately, there were no more chairs around. Freeze Palace was packed.

"I'm okay," Madison said, rocking from one foot to the other. Fiona and Egg were giggling about something. Everyone seemed to be having their own private conversations.

"I'm going for another milk shake," Drew announced. He stood up from his seat and offered it to Madison, who sat down in the middle of everyone.

"So, did you guys see what happened at the pool today?" Egg asked the table.

Everyone shook their heads. Madison knew they were talking about little Eliot's fall near the pool edge.

But they weren't.

"Ivy Daly almost lost her top," Egg cracked. "Again. She is so weird."

"And hot," Chet added. "I think she does it on purpose."

"Eeeeew, gross me," Aimee said. "She is not hot. She is so fake."

Madison couldn't believe they were talking about Ivy and not her. She looked over at Hart, but he was still too busy arm wrestling to notice.

"I was at the pool today," Madison said.

"Yo, I didn't see you," Egg said. "Oh, wait. Maybe I did. I can't remember."

Hart still said nothing.

Madison shifted uncomfortably in her seat. Her skirt felt tight all of a sudden. She was dressed up more than the rest of the group, too. The patchwork skirt had been a bad idea. She should have stayed in shorts.

"Are you guys ready for Pool Day?" Egg asked.

"I'm diving," Dan said. He was a good swimmer.

"Me too," said Fiona. She was always up for an athletic challenge. "And I'm doing the crawl against my brother."

"Breaststroke-and-backstroke combo is my swim," Hart said. "And the lifeguard swim, too, of course."

"I'll watch," Aimee said. She still wasn't ready to get her hair wet.

Madison sat back and listened to the table talk about Pool Day. There was nothing to add. She wouldn't be participating like they would be, thanks to Eliot. Not only was he causing her anxiety because of what she did—but he also caused her anxiety because of what she *couldn't* do!

"What about you, Maddie?" Dan asked. "Aren't you swimming? You almost won the crawl last year."

Madison shrugged. "I can't do Pool Day. I have to baby-sit."

"Isn't that a bummer?" Aimee said. "It won't be the same without you."

"Why don't you just blow off baby-sitting for that one day?" Egg said. "You can swim in Pool Day, win a ribbon, and be back to baby-sit after that."

"I can't," Madison said.

"It's too bad you'll miss it," Hart said. "It only happens once every summer. And we'll all be there."

Madison shrugged. "I know. . . ."

Drew walked back with his super-size milk shake and squeezed past Egg and Fiona to get back to the place he'd been sitting before. Of course, Madison was still sitting there. When he pushed through, he lost his balance.

Splooooooch.

In the blink of an eye, Madison was drenched in pink milk shake.

She sat stunned.

"I can't believe I did that," Drew said frantically. He grabbed a handful of paper napkins and pressed them onto Madison. They stuck to her blouse.

"It's not just sticky—" Madison said, standing up. "It's cold, too. Oh, gross."

"You look good," Egg said.

Madison hit him, which sent a spray of strawberry milk shake flying in all directions.

"Incoming!" Dan joked, ducking behind the table.

Everyone started to laugh.

"It isn't funny!" Madison said, crawling over Fiona to get away from the table. She hustled as fast as she could to get to the bathroom at the back of Freeze Palace.

She had to run away.

Luckily, no one was inside the bathroom. Madison stared at her splattered reflection in the bathroom mirror. She was covered in shake. Her ruffles were ruined. She turned on the faucet. This would take some time to clean up.

As she stood watching the water run until it was warm, Madison began to shake a little. Then the tears came.

"Maddie!"

Aimee opened the bathroom door and scuttled inside with Fiona.

"Maddie, are you all right?"

Madison bowed her head to keep her BFFs from seeing her cry. But she couldn't hide it for very long.

Fiona stroked Madison's hair and helped her mop off some of the pink shake. "That was such a dumb thing Drew did," she said.

"Yeah, I can't believe he spilled the whole thing. He's really embarrassed," Aimee said.

Madison wrung out the wet shirt into the sink and wiped her eyes.

"It's not the shake, really," she sobbed. "I just . . . I can't . . ." Madison started to cry harder.

"What's wrong, Maddie?" Aimee asked.

Fiona gave her a hug. "Tell us what's the matter."

"I hate summer," Madison said. "First of all, my mom is gone to another planet practically and I'm with Dad but it's not the same and my baby-sitting job is okay like ten percent of the time but the other part is just awful because Eliot cries and whines and won't let me change his stupid diaper and then he falls at the pool today and I know his mother blames me for what happened and then I hear from you guys about Pool Day and I can't go because of my job that I hate now and everything just stinks—" She had to stop to take a breath. "You wouldn't understand," she finished.

Aimee shook her head. "Of course we would!" she said. "We're your best friends."

"I didn't know your job was so hard," Fiona said. "You never told us."

"You're never around!" Madison snapped. "I'm sorry, I didn't mean to yell, but all you ever talk about anymore is boys and lying around in the sun."

Aimee and Fiona were silent.

Madison continued. "I don't want to be mean about it. I never should have taken the baby-sitting job. It's too hard, and I can't do it."

"Maddie," Fiona said gently. "You can do it. I know you can. You *are*."

By now, the pink shake was coming out of Madison's peasant shirt. The three friends had all been wringing and wiping together.

"I didn't know how you felt," Aimee said. "I wish you told us."

"Me, too," Fiona said.

"I thought I could figure everything out by

myself. I mean, I asked my parents and even Stephanie for advice. But it's not the same as you. I should have known that," Madison said.

"Nothing is the same as your BFFs," Aimee said.

"I've actually been sort of jealous of you this summer," Fiona admitted.

Madison's eyes bugged wide. "Jealous? Of what?"

"Well, I know I made a big deal about the book-a-thon and all that. And it is a big deal. But your job is so much cooler. You're doing something so important. And little Eliot will look up to you," Fiona said.

"Wow," Madison said. "You really think that?"

"She's right," Aimee said. "I have a job at my dad's store, but I'm not helping some little kid like you."

"It's so hard." Madison sniffled. "He cries all the time. And nothing I say or do makes a difference."

"I bet it does," Fiona said. "You just haven't seen it yet."

Aimee had her purse in hand. She pulled out a comb. "Here, Maddie. Let me fix your hair again. And put on some of my strawberry-kiwi lip gloss."

"Thanks," Madison said.

"And I would much rather be with you than Egg," Fiona said.

Madison raised an eyebrow. "Oh, yeah?"

Aimee giggled.

"Okay," Fiona said. "Maybe I'd rather be with Egg. But that's only because I've been waiting for someone to like me like this forever. . . ."

Madison smiled. "It's okay, Fiona. I understand. I'm cool. I'll find someone to like eventually."

"Do you feel any better now?" Aimee asked.

Madison took a deep breath and stared back at her reflection. "Much better. I feel much better."

"Do you like Hart?" Aimee asked out of the blue.

Madison felt her whole body tighten. "Huh?" she asked.

"I know it's dumb, but the other day I heard him at the pool talking to Egg and Drew, and he was talking about you," Aimee said. "And I was just wondering, if you like him, too, then maybe . . ."

Fiona shrugged. "Wow, that's interesting."

Madison's heart was racing so fast, she thought she might pass out right there on the bathroom floor. Without knowing it, Aimee had just said the one thing that was a surefire way to cheer Madison up. It was something she'd wanted to hear for as far back as she could remember.

Hart had been talking about her.

Even though this was a huge opportunity to reveal all, Madison continued to deny her crush. She felt uncomfortable about giving away her biggest secret. She would continue to keep it safe inside her files and e-mails to Bigwheels only.

"Sorry. That was a dumb thing to say. Hart is nice,

but . . ." Aimee said. "Ivy Daly has her eye on him, anyhow."

"Yeah, well," Madison said, desperate to change the subject for fear that her true feelings would start leaking out. "Um . . . should we be going back now?"

"Can I buy you an ice cream?" Fiona asked Madison.

"Yum! Let's get a big one and split it," Aimee said.

"Nah," Madison said. "Let me buy you an ice cream. The one good thing about baby-sitting is that I've made some money for my savings account. So it's *my* treat, okay?"

"Okay, I'll take an ice cream," Fiona said.

"Yeah, why not?" Aimee said. "You're rich."

Madison laughed. "Yeah, right."

At the counter, Madison ordered a few cones, and then the trio returned to the table with the boys. Of course, Drew apologized a hundred times for spilling the shake. And of course, Madison forgave him a hundred times.

Eight o'clock rolled around soon, and Dad came by the Freeze Palace to pick up Madison. He walked her home slowly, the two of them enjoying the last bits of blue and yellow and pink light in the sky.

Madison got ready for bed as soon as she arrived home. Tomorrow was a big day. She crawled into bed with Phin and her laptop and booted up her files.

Pool Day

Rude Awakening: Friends are like fortune cookies. The best part is on the inside.

Aimee and Fiona were SO great in the bathroom @ Freeze Palace. I didn't expect to lose it like that. I guess I've been keeping a lot hidden from them. Why do I do that?

When I got back, Mom called like she's been trying to do every night. I miss her so much when she travels. I don't think she knows how much. I hate it when she isn't available to take care of me. I need her so much sometimes. It's hard to admit that.

I can't believe I got so upset tonight about stupid Pool Day! But in some ways, this summer has been like being in the deep end of the pool.

But I won't sink, will I?

Chapter 12

"Maddie?" There was static on the phone line, so Madison didn't recognize the voice at first.

"Mom?" she said into the receiver.

It was seven-thirty in the morning in Far Hills, which meant that it was nearly midnight in Australia.

"I know today is the day of the swimming races, and I wanted to wish you good luck," Mom said.

"But I'm not racing, Mom," Madison said. "Don't you remember? Eliot is going, and I'm watching him race."

"Exactly. I called because I *did* remember," Mom said. "I just wanted to say that I have a feeling today will turn out to be a special day for both of you."

"Thanks, Mom," Madison said. It was so good to hear her voice.

"I can't wait to see you," Mom said. "I'll be home on Saturday."

"I can't wait, either," Madison said.

They said their good-byes quickly. The clock was ticking, and Madison had to hurry to meet Mrs. Reed for the day. They were meeting at Lake Dora instead of the Reed house.

"Rowrroororooroo!"

Phinnie jumped up on his hind legs and begged for a Toasty-O. He caught one in midair. Madison rubbed the remaining sleep out of her eyes and took a big swig of orange juice.

Soon enough, she and Dad were on their way.

The pool area at Lake Dora was decorated in honor of Pool Day. There were streamers and balloons and loudspeakers and posters and kids *everywhere*. The Pool Day theme was "Tropicana," so the staff had put up fake palm trees and little paper umbrellas. The snack shop staff, decked out in leis, served pineapple and mango snow cones.

With all of the people rushing around, it was hard at first to see Mrs. Reed, Becka, and Eliot. Lucky for Madison, someone else saw her first.

"Maddie!" Eliot cried from across the pool area. She grinned at him and rushed to say her good morning to Mrs. Reed.

"I'm leaving for the doctor with Becka in about a

half-hour," Mrs. Reed explained. "Don't forget. Eliot's competing in the kickboard kiddie swim later on. I think I'll be back for it."

"Okay," Madison said.

"I put Eliot's horsey in the bag. It just needs to be reinflated. I also put in an extra set of clothes and sneakers," Mrs. Reed said.

"Sure thing," Madison said.

Eliot tugged on Madison's hand. "Pool, pool," he chanted. He liked watching everyone around the pool set up for the various swims and competitions. The area was more crowded than Madison had ever seen it. That kept Eliot distracted. Madison didn't have to deal with any of his fussy tears—yet.

Lake Dora staff members sent families to wait and mingle in areas *outside* the main pool deck. All of the chairs had been removed and placed on the beach by Lake Dora. Madison spotted Aimee and Fiona there and waved them over.

"Hey," Fiona said, running up to Eliot. "Are you swimming today?"

Eliot nodded. "Kickbad thwimming."

"They have this kickboard swim for the little kids," Madison translated.

"Wow," Aimee said. "That must be fun. How old are you, Eliot?"

Eliot looked up at Madison and held out his fingers. "How many birthdays?"

Madison whispered into his ear. "I'm two half,"

he said proudly, holding up three bent fingers.

"You're so big," Aimee said, smiling.

Unfortunately, Madison's BFFs couldn't hang around for long. Fiona was meeting her swim group by the other side of the pool area, and Aimee had volunteered to organize and help pass out the winners' ribbons.

"See you later on," Madison said.

Aimee and Fiona waved to Eliot. "Bye-bye!"

Eliot grabbed Madison's leg. She couldn't really move when he did that, but Madison didn't mind.

"YOUR ATTENTION, PLEASE," a voice bellowed over the loudspeaker. "THE MAIN POOL EVENTS ARE POSTED AT THE LAKE DORA SOUTH AND NORTH ENTRANCES. PLEASE REMAIN OUTSIDE THE PERIMETER OF THE POOL DURING THESE EVENTS. BLEACHERS HAVE BEEN SET UP FOR GUESTS."

Madison directed Eliot over toward the bleachers so they could sit down and play until his big event happened. On the walk over, she bumped into Hart, Egg, and Drew. They were all wearing tropical colored T-shirts in orange and yellow.

"Nice T-shirts," Madison quipped.

"Finnster," Hart said. "What's up?"

Madison felt giddy when he said hello. All she could think about was what Aimee had said the night before.

"Not much," Madison replied. "Eliot is here. He's feeling much better since yesterday's spill."

"How's it going, Eliot?" Hart asked.

"Hi!" Eliot cried. He giggled automatically.

"Hey, Maddie, your boyfriend looks cute today," Egg said, laughing.

"You know, if you're trying to be funny, Egg," Madison said, "try getting a new joke."

Hart and Drew gasped.

"Good one!" Drew said. He gave Madison a high five.

"Whose side are you on?" Egg said, punching Drew on the shoulder.

Hart snickered. "We have to go. We're referees for some of the events."

They ran off together to meet up with the other junior lifeguards.

"ATTENTION, PLEASE," the loudspeaker boomed again. "WOULD ALL PARTICIPANTS IN THE SWIM EVENTS PLEASE REPORT TO THE CLUBHOUSE FOR A PHOTO? THE EVENTS WILL BEGIN SHORTLY."

Madison searched the crowd for any more familiar faces. Eliot was standing on the bleacher next to her, eyes darting from one person to the next.

"When do we go thwimming?" he asked. "Where's Mama?"

Madison didn't know what to tell him. She pulled one of his books out of his bag and dangled it in front of him. He swatted it away.

"No! NO!" Eliot cried. "I want Mama!"

Madison wanted to shrink down to the size of a

142

pea. Was Eliot going to cry all day today? Things were going so well!

"Maddie," Eliot said. "Don't feel good."

"Huh?" Madison asked. "What's the matter?"

"Tummy ache," Eliot said. "Real bad one."

People had begun to fill in the bleacher seats. There was still plenty of room, but the area was feeling a little closed in. It was hot outside, and Madison was beginning to feel it.

"Do you want to go somewhere else?" Madison asked Eliot. She looked into his eyes. "Are you feeling sick?"

Eliot shrugged. "I wanna play with the boat."

"The boat?" Madison asked. She remembered. "Well, we can do that later, when we go home, Eliot. Right now we have to wait here until the swimming—"

"Noooooooo!" Eliot howled.

"Is everything okay?" a woman behind Madison asked. "He seems a little upset."

"Oh yes. Everything is okay," Madison said, trying to ignore the woman.

"I wanna thwim, Maddie," Eliot said again.

Madison decided to take him for another walk around the property before the swimming events began.

The contest, as it turned out, wasn't much of a contest.

For the crawl stroke, some ninth grader Madison didn't know won. Fiona and Chet competed, but neither of them won a big prize. Fiona was faster than her brother, though, which counted for something.

In diving, Dan came in second place. Madison hadn't known what a great diver and swimmer he was. When she looked way up on the diving board, even Dan looked cuter than cute. Fiona belly flopped her dive twice, but she didn't get embarrassed or anything. Poison Ivy also got a ribbon for dives, which annoyed Madison. But she had to admit Ivy was a good diver and swimmer.

Only the breaststroke-backstroke combination swim had one clear winner: Egg Diaz. He beat Hart by more than a length. Madison hadn't known what a good swimmer Egg was, either. She had to clap loudly for her best guy friend, no matter how obnoxious he was.

Aimee came and sat with Madison so they could watch a lot of the races together. By the time the Lake Dora staff got to the kiddie events, Eliot was wired on sugar. He'd eaten half a bag of cookies and drunk two juices-in-a-box, and it wasn't even lunchtime yet.

The loudspeaker finally announced the kickboard swim, and Madison breathed a sigh of relief. She followed Eliot over to the kiddie pool to compete in the event for kids two to four years old. A staff member handed out flat, red kickboards to everyone.

"Oh, goody, oh, goody," Eliot kept saying. "Look, Maddie. Surfboard."

Per Mrs. Reed's instructions, Madison pulled off Eliot's little T-shirt and checked to make sure that he was wearing enough sunblock. She checked to make sure his little bathing suit was tied, too. Eliot slid on special water wings that had been distributed by the pool staff so kids didn't sink.

"You're going to be GREAT!" Madison cheered, checking to make sure that the Band-Aid on his scrape from the day before was firmly in place.

Eliot grinned from ear to ear.

The lifeguards helped toddlers into the water. Eliot looked like he was shaking, but he got used to the water temperature. Soon he was laughing—and kicking—with everyone else.

The contest was to see who could kick and keep the water splashing the longest. Each child was assigned a lifeguard who stood behind him or her to make sure no one went under the surface.

Before the judges blew the whistle to begin, Madison felt a nudge behind her on the bleachers.

"He looks so happy," Mrs. Reed said. Becka was asleep in her arms. "We got in and out of the doctor's faster than I expected, so I rushed back here to see you both."

"Eliot's been really good today," Madison said.

"Yes, he's a good boy. I think he's just having a hard time adjusting to you-know-who," Mrs. Reed whispered, kissing Becka gently on the forehead.

"This is my friend Aimee," Madison said, introducing her to Mrs. Reed. The three were in the middle of saying hellos when the whistle blew.

Wheeeeeeeeep!

The kickboard countdown began. Eliot started smart, Madison thought. He didn't kick with all his strength right away. He splashed a little bit and then worked up speed. He was just getting in gear when half the kids were already tired and stopping.

Water splashed and sprayed everywhere. Parents flashed cameras. Lake Dora staffers kept people as far from the pool as possible for safety reasons. It sounded like a thousand birds flapping their wings.

"Go, Eliot! Go, Eliot!" Madison and Aimee cried above the crowd noise.

In the pool, Eliot powered his little legs as fast as he could. He was laughing hysterically. The race was between him, a boy with blond curly hair, and one girl in braids. Eliot was the youngest.

"Go, Eliot! Go, Eliot!" Madison and Aimee yelled again.

But then he stopped. His skin was flushed from the exercise.

"STOP YOUR ENGINES!" one lifeguard yelled. All the little kids started giggling. The gallery of watchers burst into a round of applause. As each kid exited the pool, he or she was handed a crisp blue ribbon.

"I'll be back in just a sec," Aimee said to Madison. She wanted to find Fiona—and Ben—before the lifeguard swim started.

With her arms waving wildly in the air, Madison ran over with a towel to retrieve Eliot. He was shivering a little and his bottom lip had a bluish hue, but he looked happier than happy.

"Maddie," he said, hugging the towel close. "Again! Again!"

Madison laughed. "Maybe later," she said. "Let's see your mama now."

"Mama?" Eliot asked. His eyes lit up, and he ran toward Mrs. Reed. She handed Becka to Madison for a moment and reached out to give Eliot a big hug.

Madison froze. Becka was so tiny. But although she was afraid the baby would drop right out of her arms, Madison snuggled her close and cooed in the baby's little ears. She was feeling a lot more confident about all this baby-sitting stuff.

"Mama, I was in the pool!" Eliot said proudly. He held up his blue ribbon for everyone to see. Mrs. Reed slipped his T-shirt over his head and picked him back up.

"I know, I saw you," Mrs. Reed said. "You were kicking up a storm. Isn't that a nice ribbon, honey?"

Eliot started to babble, most of which didn't sound like real English, but Madison was envious. Would he ever talk to *her* the way he spoke to his mother? After all the trauma of the week, Madison wished that she could share more in the excitement of the pool moment. But at the same time, she fully understood why Eliot would want to be with his mother instead. After all, Madison wished her own mom was here and not in Australia. Wasn't that the same thing?

Thank goodness Mom would be home soon.

"ATTENTION! PLEASE ASSEMBLE ON THE BLEACHERS FOR OUR ANNUAL LIFEGUARD SWIM-OFF. JUNIOR LIFEGUARDS WILL BE SWIMMING FIRST."

Still holding Becka in her arms, Madison whirled around to see if she saw Aimee or Fiona anywhere nearby. *Where had Aimee gone?* This was the moment of Pool Day she'd been waiting for.

"Madison," Mrs. Reed said. "I'd like to get going now. I want to get him home, and there are a few errands we need to take care of. . . ."

"Huh?" Madison looked at her, mouth open. "I'm sorry, what did you say?"

"Is all the stuff we need in these bags?" Mrs. Reed asked, gathering their belongings together. "Last time I think we left a towel here."

Becka started to squirm, so Mrs. Reed took her back.

Madison was still speechless.

"Why don't you take those bags?" Mrs. Reed went on. "I'll take the baby and Eliot. Got it? Perfect. We'll see you at the car. I'm parked in the north lot."

Mrs. Reed extended her hand, and Eliot grasped

148

onto it. He was holding his blue ribbon proudly in the opposite hand. They started to walk ahead.

Madison stood there alone with the bags.

"Um . . . um . . ." Madison said to herself as she pulled everything together and up over her shoulders. Then she saw Aimee and Fiona walking toward her.

"Maddie, what are you doing?" Aimee asked. "The lifeguard swim is starting. Why are you packing up? Where's Eliot?"

"I have to go," Madison said in a monotone voice. "Mrs. Reed left. I have to meet her right now in the parking lot."

"Are you kidding me?" Fiona asked. "But the life-guard swim is the best part of today. They have the obstacle swim and everything. You can't miss this!"

"I know," Madison said dejectedly. "I know. But I have to miss it. I have to go. Mrs. Reed—"

"Just tell her that you'll be ready to go with her in a little while. You want to see your friends swim first," Aimee said.

Madison shook her head. "I can't," she said.

A whistle blew. Madison could see the boys getting ready across the pool. Hart was shaking out his arms, and Egg was doing stretches.

"I'll see you both Saturday at the barbecue, right?" Madison said.

"Of course," Fiona said. "Oh, Maddie . . . I am so bummed. . . ."

"I'm sorry you can't stay, Maddie," Aimee said, giving her friend a little hug. "I'll E you later."

"ATTENTION! THE LIFEGUARD SWIM-OFF WILL BEGIN IN FIVE MINUTES."

Madison sighed and watched as Aimee and Fiona went to find their seats on the bleachers. She wanted to yell, cry, scream . . . do something. This didn't seem fair, after all she'd done for Eliot. Why couldn't she have this *one* thing?

She heaved the baby's bags onto her back and hobbled slowly out of the pool area—away from her friends, her crush, and one summer memory that she wouldn't get to share.

Mrs. Reed was waiting by the car. "Thank you," she said. "It was a busy day, and you made it so much easier."

"That's cool," Madison said as she loaded the bags into the car.

"It was nice to meet your friend, too. Thanks for introducing me," Mrs. Reed said.

Madison nodded. "Yeah, sure."

"I can't believe how lucky we are to have found you, Madison," Mrs. Reed said. "Eliot was just telling me that you and he had a wonderful day together."

"He said that?" Madison said. Mrs. Reed nodded.

Madison glanced inside the car. Eliot was playing with one of his bendable toys. He still hadn't let go of his blue ribbon. In the background, Madison heard a roar of applause and screaming. She knew it

150

was the lifeguard swim-off. Someone must have done something spectacular. Was Hart winning?

A part of her wished she was inside watching with her friends. But deep down, Madison knew that the swim-off wasn't where she belonged. She belonged here with Eliot. This job wasn't taking Madison away from something. It was giving her something back, something she had never experienced before.

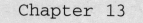

Chapter 13

 Moms

Yahoo! Mom is back!!! I have never been so happy to see her in my whole life (except of course for the last time she went away to work on a film, but anyway . . .). She's back from Australia, and she brought me these awesome shearling slippers and a funny hat and an orange belly T-shirt with a koala bear on it. She knows me so-o-o well.

Rude Awakening: Home isn't where the heart is. It's where the MOM is.

"Where are you, Maddie?" Mom called upstairs. "Didn't you hear the telephone ringing? It's Fiona!"

Madison hit the snooze function key on her lap-top and leaped off the bed.

"I'll grab it up here," Madison said. She rushed into Mom's room and clicked on the portable phone.

"Hello, Fiona?" Madison said. "What's up?"

Fiona was calling to ask if Madison wanted to come over to the barbecue a little earlier than every-one else.

"I figured if you and Aim came over soon, we could paint our nails or something. We haven't really had a chance to hang out since last weekend, right?" Fiona said. "You don't have to baby-sit or anything, do you?"

"Not today," Madison said. "I just have to check with my mom first since she just came back from her trip. But I know she'll be cool about it."

"That's great," Fiona said. "Bring some nail pol-ish so we can trade colors. I have these little adhesive stars and moons we can apply, too. I got them in this nail-decorating kit at the store."

Madison hung up and thumped downstairs to find Mom. She was busy in the kitchen making a cup of tea and pouring Phin his bowl of kibble.

"Hey, you," Mom said. "How's Fiona? Have they finished painting the house yet?"

Madison shook her head. "She was calling about the barbecue today," Madison said. "She wanted to know if I could come over earlier. Like now."

"Sure!" Mom said. "To tell you the truth,

Maddie, I think I might need to lie down and have a nap. I'm beat."

"So it's okay if I go now? You can come over later and grab some food with us," Madison said. "Mrs. Waters wanted all the moms and dads to stop by for hot dogs and hamburgers . . . well, in your case maybe just some salad."

Mom laughed. "I'll walk over after my nap. I'll call Fiona's mom to see when they light up the grill, okay?"

"Perfect!" Madison said. Normally Mom wouldn't be a cool addition to an event like this, but right now Madison could think of nothing she'd like more than to have her friends and her mom in one place.

Madison raced back upstairs and pulled on a pair of overall linen shorts, a blue shirt, and clogs. She tied back her hair in a blue ribbon with little beads on the end and applied lip gloss to make her lips shine. It tasted like berries.

Fiona had told Madison that Hart won the junior lifeguard swim-off after all. Madison wanted to look good when she waltzed right up to congratulate him on his victory.

The Waters house was in total disarray. The painting job was in full swing, and the mess of paint cans and rollers and tarps was all over the place. Madison nearly tripped on a ladder when she went up the front steps.

The paint colors were beautiful. Madison stared

and stared. Mr. and Mrs. Waters wanted to restore the shingles, trim around the windows, finials, and porch rails to the original Victorian colors. They'd picked out a deep blue and a pale yellow. It was starting to look like frosted cake.

"Hey, I did the porch," Chet announced as he opened the door. "Pretty good work, right?"

"By yourself?" Madison asked suspiciously.

Chet put his hands on his hips and squinted. "Duh, of course."

"GET AWAY FROM THE DOOR!" Fiona yelled. She pushed her brother out of the way and pulled Madison inside. "Come in! It's so hot outside!"

"Your house looks great," Madison said.

Fiona rolled her eyes. "That's because my dad and his friends were working on it. Chet washed paintbrushes or something. Loser."

"I did more than that!" Chet yelled. "Who are you calling a loser?"

"Oh, shut up," Fiona grumbled. "Come on, Maddie. Aimee's upstairs."

Fiona's room had been reorganized since Madison's last visit. Fiona still had the same Beanie Baby collection (even though those were collecting some serious dust) and her own personal purple phone, but the bed and tables were in a different place. Everything was moved to the outer walls of the room to leave a wide-open space in the center of the room for hanging out.

"Maddie!" Aimee squealed when Madison entered the room. "Welcome to Fiona's Beauty Spa and Nail Salon."

There was no air conditioner on in Fiona's room, but the windows were open wide and a mild breeze wafted inside. Madison plopped down on one of Fiona's giant pillows on the floor.

"I love your lip gloss!" Aimee said, waving her hands in the air to dry the coat of polish she'd already applied.

"Oh no! I forgot my nail polish," Madison said.

"No problem! We can just pick from these colors," Fiona said. She produced a plastic tray of polish in assorted colors. On top was the package of adhesive decals.

"So who's coming to the barbecue?" Madison said. She was hoping to hear one *H* name on the top of the list.

"All my brother's friends, including Egg, of course," Fiona said, grinning. "I think he might be coming over early, too."

"Is *Ben* coming?" Madison said, smirking.

Aimee swatted at her with the hand that was dry. "Cut it out! Why do you have to tease me about him? I don't like him that much. And I can live through one barbecue without him."

"Well, he's coming," Fiona said.

"What?" Aimee gasped. "GET OUT!"

Madison giggled.

156

"You never told me he was coming! When did you invite him? What am I going to do when he gets here? Fiona, I could kill you!"

Fiona was giggling now, too.

"Aim, you look great, quit worrying," Madison said. "I bet he's more nervous than you are."

Aimee started hopping and spinning around the room like some electronic toy gone berserk.

"Sit down and finish painting your nails," Fiona said. "No one will be here for an hour, anyway."

Madison picked out a plum color and started to apply it. "Is this too dark?" she asked her friends.

"It's perfect," Fiona said. "And you can put a little silver star on the tip, too."

Madison decided at the last minute that the plum color on her nails was way too dark and didn't match her linen shorts, so she switched manicure colors to a pale peach. The girls' nails were done and dried by the time the first guests arrived and the barbecue crowd started to appear.

Fiona and Chet had invited their friends from Far Hills Junior High, but the party also included parents, neighbors, and friends of theirs from church. In just a short time the yard and porch began to fill up with people mingling with their drinks and hors d'oeuvres. Mr. Waters and Chet had moved the ladders and paint cans into the garage.

Aimee looked out the window in Fiona's bedroom. "I see Drew! Wait! I see Egg."

"And Señora Diaz is with him," Madison said, squishing in beside Aimee at the window.

Fiona came over to see, too. "Señora Diaz and my mom have been talking lately."

"Are they talking about you and Egg or what?" Aimee asked.

"No," Fiona said, making a face. "They're just on the same parent-teacher committee at school."

The three friends ran downstairs.

"Look," Fiona cried. "Lindsay's here." Lindsay Frost was another friend from school who sometimes made a foursome out of their trio of best friends. Lindsay had been away in Europe with her family since school had been dismissed for the summer.

"You all have tans!" Lindsay cried. She gave Madison, Fiona, and Aimee big hugs.

"You look so good," Madison said. "You got your hair cut."

"I can't believe we haven't seen you in two weeks!" Aimee cried. "The summer is going by so fast already."

Mrs. Waters waded through the crowd of people in the parlor and hallway of the house, passing out stuffed mushrooms and telling guests where to find the punch and other drinks.

"This isn't the kind of barbecue I expected," Madison said. "It's like a real party."

"Yeah." Fiona shrugged. "It started out like a BBQ for Chet's friends and my friends, but then it just grew. My mom's excited to show off the house."

"Speaking of moms," Aimee said. "There's your mom, Maddie."

Madison excused herself and rushed over to say hello to Mom, who came into the party armed with flowers and a bottle of wine.

"Happy house!" Mom said cheerily as she greeted Mr. and Mrs. Waters.

Normally, Madison would have waved hello and then scooted off to be with her friends, but right now Madison was staying close to Mom's side. She stuck her arm inside Mom's arm and led her over to the table with nachos and chips.

"This place looks fantastic!" Mom said. "Hey, Maddie, maybe we should paint our house, too. What do you think?"

"I like ours the way it is," Madison said.

"Yeah, me too," Mom agreed.

"Hey, Finnster," Hart said, walking right up to Madison and Mom.

Madison jumped when she heard Hart's voice.

"Hart!" she said, feeling her cheeks blush as usual. "Um . . . this is my mom . . . I think you met before. . . . Maybe not . . ."

"Hi, Mrs. Finn," Hart said.

Mom grinned. "Hello."

Hart smiled. Then he walked off in the direction of Chet, Egg, Drew, Dan, and some other boys. They were headed outside for a game of football or Frisbee. Madison wasn't sure which. Of course, Fiona wanted to follow them outside so she could keep an eye on Egg. Aimee was frantically searching the crowd for Ben, who still hadn't arrived.

Madison decided to stay inside for a while longer with Mom. They shared a big plate of nibbles together, and Mom talked about her trip to Australia with some other neighbors, including Aimee's mom and dad, who arrived late.

The barbecue continued for hours. Madison eventually found her way outside to her friends and Hart and the rest of the boys. By now, the sports games had concluded and they were trying to start up a game of charades. Chet was making a big deal about playing flashlight tag, too, but no one could do that until it got darker outside.

Many of the parents and neighbors were leaving and the barbecue was turning into a kids-only affair. Madison's mom waved to her from the driveway. "See you at home!" she said.

Madison couldn't believe she'd survived a week of no Mom and time without friends. Today she was making up for *all* of it.

Now she just had to figure out a way to get Eliot on her side before Monday rolled around and she started work again at the Reed house.

Chapter 14

Madison spent all of Sunday with Mom in the garden. They went to the Far Hills nursery together in the morning to pick out perennials for planting. It was late in the season, but they still managed to find some colorful flowers for the side yard. Of course all Madison could think about when she was digging her fingers into the dirt was Eliot. She imagined him sitting beside her, playing with the mud the way he played with his toy boat.

Her brain was whizzing with new ideas about how to entertain Eliot and keep him happy for the rest of the summer. So what, Madison tried to tell herself, if he doesn't ever warm up to me completely?

Sunday night, Madison reopened her files and logged online.

Eliot

Rude Awakening: A mother's helper's work
is never done. Even when I'm not baby-sitting,
I'm THINKING about baby-sitting.

New ideas for Eliot and me this week:
hide-and-seek? Build the highest Lego
building? Go to the small playground down
the street? I want to try everything I can
so Eliot has a good time. And make Mrs.
Reed happy, too!

**While Madison was writing in her files, her
e-mailbox beeped. She had new mail all the way
from Bigwheels and horse camp.**

From: Bigwheels
To: MadFinn
Subject: How's Babyspitting?
Date: Sun 29 June 7:31 PM
Everyone hogs the computers @ camp
at night when we have free time!!!
Sorry I haven't written in a while.
Our days are packed with trail
riding and even some gymkhana like
having a rodeo. Mostly I just do my
best to stay on my horse (LOL), but
a guide helps me out.

Tonight was our first big Sunday,
so they had a chuck-wagon dinner

for everyone. I think I've already
found someone to like, too. Yeah! A
guy in my trail group was talking
to me @ dinner and he had the
coolest green eyes. He lives in
Idaho, so I guess we'll just be
friends while we're here unless he
becomes my keypal just like u!

Of course no one is like YOU!!! :>)

Thanx for sending ur e-mails about
the job. It's important. I'm sad u
didn't get to see Hart swim this
week, but I'm sure you'll see more
of him this summer. He prob.
understands y u missed it. BTW:
Take a picture of u & Eliot and
send it 2 me @ camp, ok? I want to
see what he looks like. Write back
soon, babyspitter! LOL.

Yours till the trail mixes,

Vicki, aka Bigwheels

Madison realized after reading Bigwheels' e-mail
that she didn't have any photos of herself and Eliot.
She would bring the digital camera and ask Mrs.
Reed to take a picture. Then she could download it
into her files and send Dad and Gramma Helen a
copy, too.

Monday morning, Madison packed the camera in with her towel and bathing suit in case the Reeds went to the Lake Dora pool again. Unfortunately, the sky looked kind of ominous, so she wasn't sure that swimming would be in the plans. But Madison wasn't going to let this rainy day get her down like she had before.

Madison ate breakfast with Mom and then left the house, skipping along the street up to the Reed house. It wasn't raining yet! Madison lived so close to Eliot—and the walk there was so easy. She could probably even bring Phin over for a visit sometime.

The front screen door at the Reeds' house was open when Madison arrived. She walked right in.

"Hello?" Madison called out.

"Madison! Good morning!" Mrs. Reed called back from another room. "I'm in here with Becka. I think Eliot's upstairs waiting for you."

Madison yelled, "Good morning," put down her bag, and looked up the stairs.

"Eliot?" Madison said. "Are you up there?"

She heard nothing. Peanut Butter and Jelly scooted down the stairs, chasing after each other. Madison climbed up.

"Eliot?" Madison asked again.

"HIYA!" Eliot screamed, popping out from behind a corner.

Madison nearly jumped out of her skin. She clutched at her chest.

Eliot roared with laughter. He swatted at her leg.

Madison smiled even though she wasn't sure what he was up to. "How are you this morning?" she asked cautiously.

"Kitties!" Eliot cried, pointing to the cats. They returned up the stairs and quickly disappeared into his bedroom. "Come on, let's go now!"

Eliot grabbed Madison's arm and started to drag her into his room. He'd never done this before. Usually he wanted his mama or he wanted to play alone. Instead of being instantly delighted, however, Madison questioned his motives.

"Do you have something in your room?" she asked. "Are the kitties playing there?"

He shook his head. "No!"

"Okay. Well, are your trucks in the bedroom?" Madison asked.

"No!" he snapped.

Madison half expected something to bonk her on the head or come crashing into her side as she walked in. Eliot was acting stranger than strange.

"My secret," he whispered. "Seeeeee-kret!"

"Secret?" Madison asked. Now she was really curious.

Eliot slowly pushed open his door. Nothing about the room looked that different than it had the week before. His small red table and chairs were still in the corner. The airplane mobile was still hanging from the ceiling. Books of all sizes were perched on a high shelf.

"What is it, Eliot?" Madison asked. "You're being awfully—"

"BOO!" Eliot cried. Madison guessed that was his way of announcing a surprise. He threw open the closet door. "My secret place."

Madison's eyes flitted in every direction. The closet was crowded with toy animals in all shapes and sizes. There was more than the typical stuffed bears and rabbits. Eliot had rhinoceroses and elephants and ten different kinds of monkey. They were arranged in rows.

"Wow! Is this your own zoo or what?" Madison asked.

"Zoo! Zoo!" Eliot chirped. "My friends. You my friend?"

Madison dropped down onto the carpet and crossed her legs so she could give Eliot her undivided attention.

"I am definitely your friend," Madison said.

"Did you meet Zebra?" he asked, distracted again. He introduced Madison to Camel, Armadillo, Cobra, and Stegosaurus Dinosaur, too. Madison was sure there were one hundred animals in here, in all shapes and sizes. She wondered why Eliot was sharing them with her now.

Then she realized why exactly.

Eliot liked Madison. And he really *did* want to be friends. Madison grinned. Even better was the fact that he liked *animals*, too. Just like Madison.

166

The two stayed upstairs for over and hour, taking animals out of the closet and examining their coats and scales and tails. It was quite a collection.

After the morning flew by, Madison and Eliot headed downstairs to have a snack and some lunch. Before they ate, they fed the Reed cats together. Eliot liked petting Peanut Butter while she lapped her milk.

"Do you like her tongue?" Madison asked. She put a drop of milk on Eliot's hand so the cat would lick the milk off.

"Ooh!" Eliot laughed. "Tickles."

"I should bring my doggy over so you can meet him," Madison suggested.

"DOGGY!" Eliot squealed.

After lunch, Eliot didn't need much entertaining. He was content to sit on the window seat and stare at the rain. As droplets rolled down, he tried to catch them from behind the glass. "Wain!" he cried.

Madison gave him a surprise hug as they sat there. She expected Eliot to wriggle away, but he didn't. He rested his head on her shoulder. It was nap time and he wasn't putting up a fight? Normally, Mrs. Reed put Eliot down for daily naps, but today it appeared that Eliot was ready to have Madison take over that task. He snuggled closer.

"Maddie?" Eliot said. "Thwimming! Thwim!"

"Oh, I'm sorry. We can't go to the pool today," Madison explained. "It's wet and hot outside. We have to stay in here."

"Nonononono!" Eliot said, shaking his head. "Thwim!"

Eliot pushed away from Madison, and she felt a pang of dread. Was he running away again? He climbed down off the window seat and tottered away into the other room.

"Eliot?" Madison cried out. "Come back here, Eliot. We have stuff to do. "

No answer. Madison wondered if maybe he was originating a game of hide-and-seek all on his own. She walked through the house, looking for his little orange socks—the one article of clothing that might give him away. Was he hiding behind the sofa? Back up in his closet? Madison didn't know.

"Eliot?" she asked aloud.

"Is everything okay in here?" Mrs. Reed said, appearing at the doorway with Becka in her arms. Becka's face was smeared with formula and apple-sauce. She quietly looked around.

"I think Eliot's playing a game of hide-and-seek," Madison explained.

No sooner had she said that, however, than Eliot reappeared. He was holding something behind his back.

"What are you up to?" she asked, picking him up.

Eliot grinned. "Here!" he said. In his small fist he was holding on to something. Madison peeled apart his fingers.

It was the blue ribbon he'd won at Pool Day.

"Look, it's Eliot's prize!" Madison cheered.

"No!" Eliot yelled, shaking his head. He pushed the ribbon into Madison's face.

"Looks like he wants someone else to have that ribbon," Mrs. Reed said.

Madison looked at Eliot. "Eliot's ribbon," she said clearly.

Eliot giggled. "I want down," he said.

Madison lowered him to the ground and held the ribbon out and away for herself.

"Maddie ribbon!" Eliot said.

"Did you tell him to give me this?" Madison asked Mrs. Reed, who quickly shrugged "no." She was smiling, admiring her son.

"Wow, Eliot," Madison said. She had one of those lumps in her throat. Only this wasn't a bad-omen lump. This was a *very good* lump.

Here was what Madison had been waiting for since she'd started baby-sitting.

"Thank you, thank you," Madison said a few times in a row.

Eliot seemed pleased with himself. He grabbed Madison's arm and swung it from side to side.

Mrs. Reed looked doubly pleased. "Well, some-one has a new friend. That's for sure." She looked as surprised as Madison.

Right on cue, Becka cooed.

After lunch Madison and Eliot played with the animals, read animal stories, and laughed together.

169

Madison had never had such a great time at the Reed house. She told Eliot all about endangered animals and volunteering at the animal clinic even though she was certain he didn't understand what either of those things were.

By the late afternoon, Madison asked Mrs. Reed for some blank paper and crayons. She set them out on the table and invited Eliot to color along with her. First they drew a picture of the family—Mr. Reed, Mrs. Reed, Eliot, Becka, Peanut Butter and Jelly. That picture went up on the refrigerator. Then they drew a picture for Becka. Eliot drew funny bunnies with extra-long ears. At least that's what Madison said they were. They could have been almost anything, since it was really only a bunch of squiggles.

Madison wished they could have made a collage of scraps and photos, but she'd save that for another time. There was plenty of time to make new memories with Eliot.

When Madison left for the day, she was brimming with pride. She wanted to give him a ten-minute hug and thank him for making her wish come true. But Eliot wasn't in the mood for hugs. He was too distracted and dashed off to find his trucks.

"See you tomorrow, Madison," Mrs. Reed said. "Thanks again. I think we really turned a corner today. Eliot seems to have really warmed up to you."

Madison nodded. "I know." Her face felt flushed. "See you tomorrow."

She walked slowly down the steps of the Reed house and onto the street. She watched as a fleet of about six kids rode their bikes through the puddles on the street. Everyone who'd been cooped up all day was outside now to enjoy the evening. The rain had stopped an hour earlier, but it hadn't cooled anything down. The air was very sticky and hot. Thankfully, home was only minutes away.

As she turned down Blueberry Street, Madison ran into Aimee, who was out walking Blossom.

"Maddie!" Aimee yelled, running up the street. "Howdy! Where were you?"

Madison beamed. "Work."

"Oh no, was Eliot a troublemaker again today?" Aimee asked.

Madison shook her head. "Nope. He was perfect."

"Perfect?" Aimee laughed. "There is no boy in the world who's perfect!"

Madison laughed at the joke, and they walked on down the block.

Of course she knew the truth.

Right now, Eliot was about as close to perfect as she could have imagined. And she couldn't wait to baby-sit him tomorrow.

Mad Chat Words:

:-V	Giving you a shout out
(((((:-{=	He's a rave dude
:**(	Sniffle, sniffle
%-Z	Doofy
RUKM?	Are you kidding me?
OC	Of course
QT	Cutie
HUP	Heads up
sitch	Situation
IIWM	If it were me . . .
FYA	For your amusement
NT	Not true
ONNA	Oh no, not again

Madison's Computer Tip

I don't know what I would have done these past weeks if I hadn't had my keypal. Thanks to Bigwheels and the Internet, I got all the baby-sitting and friend advice I needed. Things with Eliot worked out much better. Why should I be stressed out about not knowing something when all this cool information is at my fingertips? **I can look up just about anything online—and learn so many new things in a matter of minutes.** If only I could surf the Internet for swimming tips—and learn how to do a better crawl stroke! Then I'd really be happy—LOL.

Visit Madison at www.madisonfinn.com

172